AGENT ARTHUR'S DESERT CHALLENGE

Martin Oliver

Illustrated by
Paddy Mounter

Designed by
Paul Greenleaf

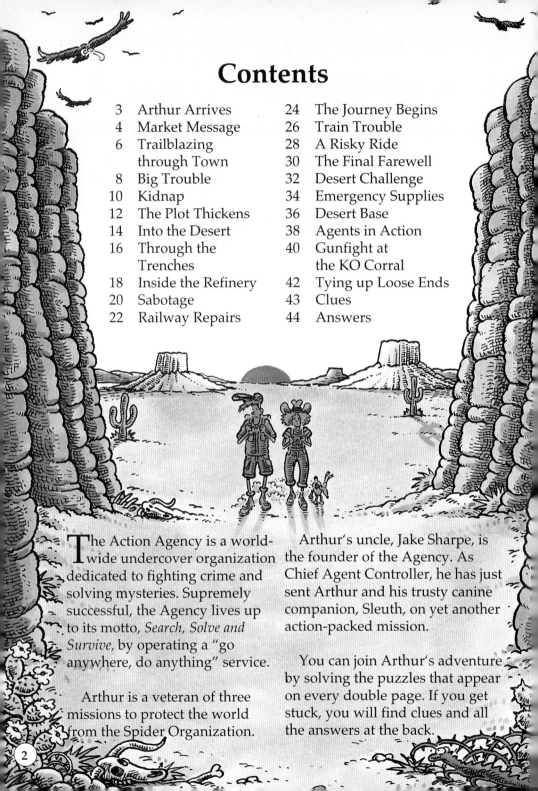

Contents

The Action Agency is a world-wide undercover organization dedicated to fighting crime and solving mysteries. Supremely successful, the Agency lives up to its motto, *Search, Solve and Survive*, by operating a "go anywhere, do anything" service.

Arthur is a veteran of three missions to protect the world from the Spider Organization.

Arthur's uncle, Jake Sharpe, is the founder of the Agency. As Chief Agent Controller, he has just sent Arthur and his trusty canine companion, Sleuth, on yet another action-packed mission.

You can join Arthur's adventure by solving the puzzles that appear on every double page. If you get stuck, you will find clues and all the answers at the back.

Arthur Arrives

The travelling lasso-seller's cart creaked to a halt in a busy street in a dusty desert town.

"Welcome to El Taco, gateway to the desert," Agent Arthur murmured as he jumped off. "Stay alert Sleuth, we're on active service now."

Sleuth sniffed around suspiciously while Arthur tried to forget about his disastrous lassoing lessons and struggled to remember the contents of his mission dossier.

"We must head for the main square," Arthur said. "Any ideas where it is?"

Market Message

A few minutes later, Arthur followed Sleuth into the bustling main square. It was market day. Arthur took in all the strange sights and sounds and headed straight for the lively stalls.

"This is a good time to buy a desert disguise," he whispered to Sleuth. "You never know when we may need to blend seamlessly into the background. What do you think of this?"

Sleuth snorted in disgust but Arthur was proud of his new purchases. He was admiring his sombrero when he suddenly noticed a piece of paper clipped to the brim. The paper was covered in a series of unmistakable symbols – it was an Action Agency message.

What does the message say?

Trailblazing Through Town

After decoding the message, Arthur glanced around casually. The shady sombrero seller had disappeared. Now to dispose of the message.

As he waved it at Sleuth, Arthur felt warm breath over his shoulder and turned to see teeth chomping into the note.

"Yikes," yelled Arthur. He jumped out of the munching mule's way, slipped, and landed up-ended beneath a fruit stall. A street plan of El Taco fluttered gently out of his battered hat.

"Just what I was looking for," Arthur smiled groggily. "Now to meet our contact, Agent Andrea."

"This way," Arthur said, getting unsteadily to his feet. "Come on."

Sleuth reluctantly followed behind as Arthur strode down an alley and turned left.

"This map reading's so easy," Arthur thought confidently. He took the next right, skirted carefully past a cactus salesman and followed the alley as it led . . . back to the market.

"It's er . . . all part of my Action Plan to confuse onlookers," Arthur mumbled. "Which way now?"

Sleuth wagged his tail and set off. Giving a mule trader a wide berth, Arthur followed Sleuth out of the square and down narrow streets.

"Nothing must distract us from our mission," Arthur whispered. "We mustn't waste any time."

Just then they walked past a food stall. Arthur stared hungrily at the snacks on display. Surely one mouthful wouldn't hurt. Ignoring Sleuth's warning growls, Arthur picked up a dish and took a huge mouthful. Everything went red!

growl!

Arthur blazed a trail over to a pump and gulped down gallons of water. At last the fire inside him was out. Now he could get back to his mission. But before he set off he thought back to the warning in the Action Agency message. Arthur sensed that something was wrong.

he he!

What has Arthur noticed?

Big Trouble

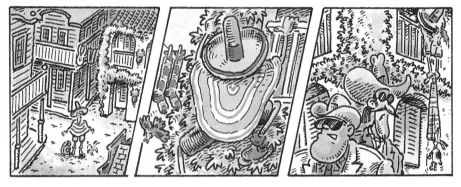

A rthur sprang into evasion mode. He raced down an alley until he reached a crossroads.

Which way should he go? Arthur had a great idea. Quick as a flash, he clambered up a drainpipe and onto a balcony.

But Sleuth was in trouble. Using his poncho, Arthur hauled him up. Just in time! Two shady figures appeared below them.

We've lost him. Where can he have gone? We must find him.

The boss won't be very happy. What do you think we can do?

Wishing his heart would stop beating so loudly, Arthur cautiously peered over the balcony. Directly below were the characters who had been on his trail.

Arthur remembered his mission instructions as he listened to the muttered conversation. The two men had to be Scorpion Mobsters, but who was their boss?

At that moment a tall figure marched menacingly up to the men. Sleuth's hackles rose and Arthur gulped as he recognized the woman. He had come up against her before. Arthur ducked down as he thought back to her Crookfax. Bella Donna was big trouble.

Arthur had to stay hidden until the villains had gone. But as he crept back out of sight, he knocked a flowerpot off the balcony ...

Arthur waited for the angry shouts and gunshots, but nothing happened. He looked down and saw one of the Scorpion Mobsters out cold. Bella Donna and the other man had disappeared. Arthur and Sleuth jumped to the ground to check the damage.

Apart from a bump on his head, the villain was all right. Two pieces of paper had fallen out of his pockets. They could be vital. Sleuth checked that the coast was clear while Arthur began reading.

What does the message say?

9

Kidnap

Arthur was still trying to take in all the information he had decoded when he found that he had stumbled across the meeting place. There was a figure waiting by the statue of Il Desperado holding a red crash helmet – it had to be his contact, Agent Andrea.

Just then a car screeched to a halt. Arthur thought back to the Mobster's coded message. "Look out," he shouted, but it was too late. A bang echoed in Arthur's ears and a cloud of gas enveloped the statue.

Through the smoke, Arthur could just make out Agent Andrea being dragged into the car by two gas-masked men. The engine roared.

Arthur's brain raced. He pulled something out of his bag and sprinted over to the car. The woman behind the wheel was none other than Bella Donna! She snarled angrily and drove straight at Arthur.

At the last second Arthur dived out of the way. As he flew through the air, his right hand brushed the side of the car.

He hit the dirt, rolled over, and watched the car speed away in a cloud of dust. Sleuth was about to bound after the rapidly retreating villains when he felt Arthur grab his collar.

"Don't worry, they won't get away," Arthur muttered grimly, getting to his feet. "I had a little trick up my sleeve. I planted a radio beacon on their car."

Sleuth looked on in amazement as Arthur rooted through his bag and produced an electronic gadget.

"It's a top-secret tracking device, developed by Uncle Jake," Arthur explained, hitting the 'on' button. "The red line on the screen shows the route taken by Bella Donna and her crooked cronies. Now we must trace their path on the map."

By the time Arthur had found the map, the line on the screen had stopped moving. The kidnappers must have reached their destination.

Where are they?

The Plot Thickens

Uncle Jake's tracking device was a great success, unlike Arthur's map reading. He and Sleuth were hot, dusty and thirsty by the time they had arrived at Avenida Rodeo.

"They must have hidden the car," gasped Arthur. "It has to be in that building with the green doors. There's no time to lose. Stay alert, we're going in."

Sleuth found a way in through a broken plank in a side door. He growled the all-clear and Arthur crept inside to join him.

"Bingo! There's the car. Well done, Sleuth," Arthur muttered. "Keep an eye open for Bella Donna. Once we've rescued Agent Andrea, we'll try to find out what the Scorpion Mob is planning to do next."

Just then they heard the screech of wheels outside. Arthur dashed over to the back window and saw two trucks racing off. He pulled at the door – it was stuck tight.

Arthur tugged and heaved the door open, but the villains were speeding away. As they swerved around the corner, a stream of objects fell off the last truck.

"We're too late!" Arthur gasped. "They've gone."

Arthur had to follow, but where were they going? He looked around at all the empty boxes and open drawers and his heart sank. Bella Donna had done a good job at clearing up her operation.

Suddenly Sleuth barked, and pawed at something. It was a red crash helmet – the one Agent Andrea had been carrying. Arthur picked it up. It was much heavier than he expected, unless . . .

"It must be a special Action Agency helmet," he said, tearing open the inner lining. Photos, a diary and two coded messages came spilling out.

"This must be Agent Andrea's vital information. I have a hunch that it will tell us where Bella Donna is heading."

What do the papers say?
Where is Bella Donna heading?

Into the Desert

Arthur now knew where the Scorpions were heading and he was certain that they had taken Andrea with them. If he gave chase, he could rescue his fellow agent and maybe foil the Scorpion Mob's attack too.

But before Arthur could move, Sleuth dropped something at his feet. It was a stone-like object with a cactus shape in it that had fallen off the back of the villains' truck. What could it be? There was no time to ponder the question now. They had to locate the jeep that Andrea had mentioned in her log.

They found it easily. Arthur checked the survival equipment in the back, then he pulled out his Action Agency Any-Ignition Key and started the engine.

He stamped on the accelerator and the jeep lurched forward. Sleuth clung on desperately as they raced through the streets.

"Don't worry," Arthur said. "There's only one road out of El Taco. We'll soon catch them."

Arthur's confidence quickly dried up in the desert heat. A burning breeze blew sand toward the jeep, making it difficult to see. An hour out of town, the road turned into a dirt track. As Arthur swerved to avoid the potholes, he didn't notice the maps flying off the back of the jeep.

On and on they drove. Arthur followed the road ahead while Sleuth kept a look-out for signs of Bella Donna and her cronies.

They jolted along, and were nearing a crossroads, when suddenly the wheels on the jeep blew out.

They skidded to a halt and Arthur staggered out. The blow-out had buckled the axle and the jeep was beyond repair. On the road Arthur saw shards of glass.

"This is Bella Donna's work," he muttered. "But she won't stop us."

Arthur was about to search for the maps when he spotted Sleuth by the remains of a signpost. He dashed over to him and quickly realized the way that they should go to get to the refinery.

Which way is it?

Through the Trenches

Arthur packed a basic survival kit in a backpack and they set off. Sweat poured off his brow as he followed Sleuth down the rough track. Two hours and ten bottles of water later, they were still trekking as the sun beat down on the dusty duo.

"We must be nearly there," Arthur groaned between swigs of water. "Stay on red alert."

Just then Sleuth sniffed the air and growled. He bounded off the road and crept up a stony ridge. Arthur followed close behind him.

Arthur shielded his eyes as he scanned the scene. Down below, the channels of a river had dried up, forming a series of trenches. On the other side, they could see the refinery, guarded by Scorpion sentries. Beyond a wire fence, Bella Donna was striding into a hut.

"We must get into the refinery," muttered Arthur. "We can easily reach the wrecked truck, but then we need to find a safe route through the trenches and past the fence."

Can you find a safe route into the refinery?

Inside the Refinery

Sleuth bounded happily along the pipe that led under the fence while Arthur crawled after him.

"Be careful," he warned Sleuth. "Once we're out of here, we're in Scorpion territory."

Arthur squinted in the bright sunlight as they leaped out of the pipe. Keeping out of sight of the guards, he and Sleuth hurdled over a steel tube, raced over the sand and hit the dirt behind some rusty oil drums.

Welcome to the Scorpion Mob. I have a gift for you and Andrea.

aargh!

Bella Donna smiled evilly as Arthur was pushed into the hut. She hissed a strange welcome then thrust something under his nose. Arthur stared at two Scorpion ID cards – with his and Andrea's photos on them!

"You've fallen into my trap," Bella Donna gloated. "By the time you're found, my plan will have been a complete success."

Arthur heard a hiss of gas and everything went black.

Arthur peered through the window of the hut he had seen Bella Donna entering. She was holding a piece of paper in one hand and talking in urgent tones. Arthur listened carefully to what she was saying to her henchman.

Arthur ignored Sleuth's warning growl. He was so busy trying to get a closer look that he didn't notice his faithful companion disappear with the backpack, or the dark shadow behind him, until it was too late . . .

At last Arthur came to. He rubbed his eyes and gasped. The hut had been wrecked. In one hand was his fake ID card, by the other was a cosh. Agent Andrea was slumped on the floor. Arthur knew things were terribly wrong.

Then he spotted Andrea's fake ID and the paper Bella Donna had been holding. If he could decode it, things might become clearer.

What does the paper say?
What is Bella Donna's plan?

Sabotage

Arthur's brain reeled as he pocketed the fake ID cards. Bella Donna had been trying to set them up. But what was all this about destroying the refinery? That must be what Operation Smokescreen was all about.

Arthur had to bring Andrea around first. He opened the hut door and dragged her outside, just as Sleuth appeared. Arthur bent down to pat him when BOOM, CRASH, BOOM, explosions ripped through the refinery. Arthur was blown off his feet and landed beside Agent Andrea. Her eyes opened wide in surprise.

"Agent Arthur?" she gasped. "What's going on?"

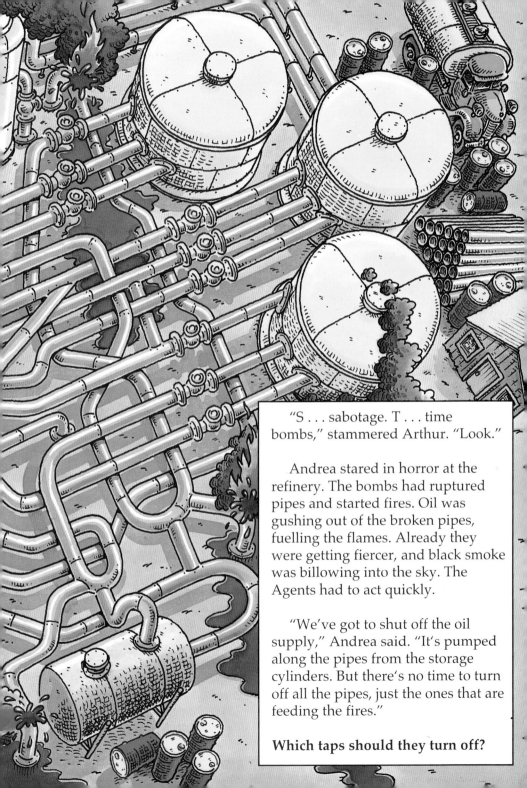

"S . . . sabotage. T . . . time bombs," stammered Arthur. "Look."

Andrea stared in horror at the refinery. The bombs had ruptured pipes and started fires. Oil was gushing out of the broken pipes, fuelling the flames. Already they were getting fiercer, and black smoke was billowing into the sky. The Agents had to act quickly.

"We've got to shut off the oil supply," Andrea said. "It's pumped along the pipes from the storage cylinders. But there's no time to turn off all the pipes, just the ones that are feeding the fires."

Which taps should they turn off?

Railway Repairs

At last Arthur and Andrea slumped down in the shade of a tall hut. It had been hot work, but they had beaten the flames.

Arthur took some swigs of water from a fire bucket, then told Andrea about Bella Donna's attempt to frame them.

Andrea turned pale when she heard the details of Bella Donna's devious plan, but then it was her turn to surprise Arthur.

"Operation Smokescreen isn't just about framing us," she began. "It's also meant to distract us from Operation Sandstorm."

I don't know the target of Operation Sandstorm. Bella Donna joked about a "training" mission, but that's all I heard.

A dust cloud could be seen on the horizon, heading their way.

"Help at last," said Arthur. But then an awful thought struck him. "What if the Agency has decoded the fake message and sent back-up Agents," he breathed. "We'll have a great deal of explaining to do."

"And by the time we've told them Bella Donna's real plans, Operation Sandstorm will have been carried out," Andrea said.

"You're right," Arthur agreed. "We'll have to thwart the operation on our own – that should prove that we're not double agents."

But first they had to escape through the desert. How could they do that when the jeep was out of action? Sleuth suddenly jumped up and dashed off.

"Follow him," Arthur yelled. "He may have an idea."

Sleuth led the agents past the charred pipes to a large shed.

"But how does this railway repair shop help us?" said Arthur.

"There's a railway line that runs from here to the coast," replied Andrea. "If we find the missing parts of this handcar, I can bolt them back into place and we can get away."

Can you find the missing parts?

Train Trouble

Arthur thought hard. Had the Scorpion Mob captured the train? Was this part of Operation Sandstorm? What was it all about?

There was only one way to find out. As the whistle blew and the train began to move, Arthur and Andrea sprinted across the sand and leaped for the guard's van.

Once they were safely aboard, Arthur came up with an Action Plan. Before Andrea could reply, he and Sleuth were gone.

They crept through the guard's van, past a sleeping henchman, and into the next carriage which was full of theatrical props, and dummies in strange costumes.

Arthur strode through the carriage but could go no further ... the door was locked. He peered into the next wagon and gasped. It was guarded by two armed mobsters and was full of glittering gold bars! So that was what the Scorpion Mob was up to. They had captured the Sandstorm Express because it was a bullion train!

> Grrr!

Just then Sleuth's hackles rose and in the distance Arthur heard someone moving around in the guard's van. The sleeping henchman must have woken up.

Arthur gulped – he was trapped. What could he do? There was no way out of the carriage without being spotted unless . . . Arthur suddenly had a brainstorm.

"What do you think?" he hissed a few seconds later. "As long as I've got the costume right, the guard will take me for a dummy, not an Action Agent."

Sleuth stared in amazement then growled. Arthur had overlooked some telltale details. He had to sort them out quickly.

What has Arthur forgotten?

A Risky Ride

Arthur held his breath and stood stock still as the villain walked past. It was all going well until the feather in Arthur's hat began to tickle his nose.

"I . . . I can explain," Arthur stuttered, but the Scorpion Mobster was in no mood to listen. He grabbed a sword, chased Arthur onto the roof and lunged.

Arthur opened his eyes in time to see Agent Andrea tying his dazed opponent to the roof.

"I don't know how you did that," gasped Arthur. "But thanks."

"That's OK," Andrea replied. "I could see that you were in trouble. Luckily none of the other guards have seen us, but why are all these Scorpion guards on this train anyway?"

Sweat poured off Arthur's brow as he parried just in time. Cold steel glinting in the bright sunlight, his opponent attacked again. Arthur fended him off.

They locked swords and Arthur was pushed back to the edge of the carriage. Soon he had nowhere left to go. The train sped on as he braced himself for the inevitable . . .

Andrea's eyes opened wide as Arthur quickly explained about the gold bullion aboard. That answered her questions, but what was their next step? How could they stop Bella Donna's operation?

"We must uncouple the train from the engine," Andrea said. "But that means getting to the engine cab without being seen."

Is there a safe route to the cab?

The Final Farewell?

After a hair-raising clamber over the train, Arthur, Andrea and Sleuth dropped into the engine cab. Nothing could go wrong now, or so they thought, but the train driver had other ideas. Arthur gulped as he stared down the barrel of Bella Donna's gun. Was it all over?

He didn't have to wait too long to find out. With Bella Donna's triumphant laugh still ringing in his ears, he felt himself flying through the air. He hit the sand then bounced and somersaulted down the embankment. On and on he rolled until he thudded into a very prickly cactus.

TOOT, TOOT. Arthur peered through watering eyes and saw Bella Donna waving from the train as it steamed off into the distance. Dustclouds marked Andrea and Sleuth's progress down the same sandy embankment.

Arthur limped over to the others. They were covered in sand but unhurt. Arthur winced as he extracted the last cactus spine from his body.

"So what do we do now?" Arthur said, as the sun blasted down on the tired trio. "Do we follow that train or just wait to be rescued?"

"Neither," Andrea replied grimly. "Bella Donna will be miles away, and it could be days before we're found. We're running out of water ... we must get more first."

Arthur knew Andrea was right – Bella Donna would have to wait. Right now the Action Agents had to work out their location, then head for the nearest oasis.

While Andrea was scribbling some journey notes, Arthur dug out his map and Agency Issue Compass. Then he began scanning the horizon for landmarks. There was no time to waste. Every second in the burning heat sapped their energy and brain power.

Where are the Action Agents?
Where is the nearest oasis?

Desert Challenge

Sunset

Night

Sunrise

Arthur blinked in the glaring sun. The nearest oasis was a day and a half's walk away. This desert trek really would be the ultimate survival challenge.

"Let's move," Andrea said, packing the backpack. "Water will be rationed until we reach the oasis. We must find some shade, then rest until it is cooler."

Arthur took a deep breath and they set off. The sun blazed down as the trio slowly made their way through the burning sands. Nothing moved in the shimmering heat, except for the Action Agents.

On and on they toiled. Arthur checked the map and compass while Andrea carried the back-pack. Only Sleuth seemed not to mind the terrible heat as he gnawed on some interesting finds.

At last they collapsed under a parched tree. Andrea trickled out their water ration. Arthur swallowed gratefully and tried to keep his mind on the task ahead.

As the sun dropped, so did the temperature. The trio set off again. All night long they stumbled through the cold, desolate landscape . . . until once again the sun rose.

Would they ever reach water? Arthur wiped the thought from his mind and, ignoring his blistered feet, staggered after the others. They hauled their aching bodies onward until at last Arthur stopped to check his map.

Where was that oasis? Arthur squinted through red eyes and spotted vultures overhead, waiting for the kill. Nervously he licked his scorched lips.

"Maybe it's over the next dune," Arthur croaked hopefully.

They staggered to the top and, to Arthur's amazement, there was the oasis. They had made it! Arthur raced down the slope and was about to dive in, when he stopped dead. The oasis was dry.

What could they do now? Andrea poured out the last drops of water in a desperate attempt to refresh their drained brain power.

"We can't go on much longer," Arthur gulped. "We need water, and we need it now."

Andrea nodded grimly. As she scanned the horizon, something reminded her of Agent Zak's desert trek. Her heart leaped. Maybe they had a chance after all.

What has Andrea remembered?

Emergency Supplies

Two sweltering hours later, the Action Agents staggered into the ramshackle fort. Sleuth sniffed around the courtyard, then he bounded through a door and into a small outbuilding. A few moments later he reappeared with an Action Agency Emergency Kit in his teeth.

Arthur rubbed his eyes. Was it a mirage? There was only one way to find out. He dived into action.

"This is delicious," Arthur sighed a few minutes later. "We couldn't have survived much longer without these supplies."

"You're right," Andrea nodded, between swigs of water. "But the supplies aren't all that Zak left. His mission log mentions Bella Donna's desert base. I bet that's where she is heading. If we reach it, we may find her, Agent Zak and the gold."

It was a good plan, but if they were to survive the next trek through the desert, they would have to recover from the last one. They rested in the shade and packed supplies. At last they were ready. Arthur took a deep breath, then they left the fort.

The sun shone down as the trio headed west. Picking their way through the spiky shrubs, they trudged through the rocky desert.

Eventually they came to a range of cliffs towering above them. At first it seemed they could go no further . . . but then Andrea remembered something.

"This is the place that Agent Zak mentioned in his log," she said excitedly. "He got through one of the gorges. If we follow his clues we'll find out which one to take."

Which gorge should they take?

Desert Base

They set off in single file through the gorge. As dawn broke, Arthur spotted a gap ahead. They had reached the end. He was about to stride on when Sleuth growled softly.

"We'd better be careful," Andrea whispered, testing footholds in the rockface. "The exit will probably be guarded. We'll take a slight detour up this slope. Follow me and don't make a sound."

A few minutes later they reached the others at the top of the rock. Andrea was right, two villains were guarding the entrance to the gorge. Below them was a ramshackle town – it had to be Bella Donna's desert base.

"We must see if Zak is down there," said Arthur. "The gold may also be in the town. It's too heavy to move from the train . . . but where could they have hidden a train?" Andrea pointed excitedly to a railway track leading into a tunnel.

A few minutes later Arthur smiled at Andrea. She had been right . . . they had found the Sandstorm Express inside an old mine at the end of the tunnel, but the bullion car was empty. Where was the gold?

The Action Agents began searching the mine, but they hadn't made much progress when . . .

They were interrupted by a menacing voice. Turning, they saw an armed guard. Had they come this far only to be captured again?

Arthur racked his brains. Then he realized that he had something that would get them out of trouble. He began to search his pockets.

What is Arthur looking for?

Agents in Action

Arthur took back the fake ID cards from the guard, then followed Andrea out of the cave.

"Now to town," he said. "We must find Bella Donna and Zak."

Trying to act casually, the trio searched the town. They spotted Bella Donna in the bank, but first they had to find Zak and the gold.

They carried on with their search, peering into the saloon on the way. Just then Andrea had a flash of inspiration. It was so obvious ... if Zak was a prisoner, he wouldn't be in the *bar*, he would be behind *bars*.

Andrea's hunch had been right, but how could they rescue him?

"I've got an Action Plan," Arthur muttered. "Just leave this to me." He flashed his fake ID and the jailer left them alone with the prisoner. Andrea unlocked Zak's cell.

"How . . . how did you? . . ." Zak began.

"It's too long a story," said Andrea. "This is Arthur and Sleuth. Do you know where the gold is?"

Zak looked puzzled. Arthur realized that they would have to search the town again.

They made for the door. Arthur stopped as he spotted a crowd of villains outside. The Action Agents braced themselves for a fight, but the Scorpion Mobsters headed past the jail and into a barn. Why?

"They've got more important things to do," Zak said. "They're going to drink homebrew. Bella Donna banned drinking but there's a secret supply in there."

"Those doors are the only way in or out," said Zak. "If we could lock or bolt them, the villains would be trapped, but how can we do it?"

How can they secure the doors?

The boss told us to take over guard duty.

Agent Andrea..!

Gunfight at the KO Corral

While Andrea and Zak bolted the barn doors, Arthur began looking for Bella Donna. This time she wasn't going to escape. Arthur was determined to find her but it was Bella Donna who found Arthur!

The bank had been empty and Arthur was heading along the main street toward the KO Corral when his arch enemy appeared. Arthur squinted into the sun and gulped when he heard her familiar voice.

Bella Donna reached for her six-shooters. In a blur of motion, she drew the guns and fired from the hip. Arthur dived out of the way just in time.

He picked himself up and, keeping low, sprinted for cover. Bullets whizzed over his head and tin cans jangled as he collided with a wooden crate.

A hail of lead followed Arthur's progress. He dived behind a water trough and ducked as bullets, boxes and bottles flew around his ears.

Suddenly the firing stopped. Arthur peered out and saw that Bella Donna was reloading her pistols. On the horizon Arthur spotted more Scorpion Mobsters coming to pick up the gold. Arthur might just be able to take care of Bella Donna, but first he had to divert the newcomers.

What could he do? As Arthur racked his brains he glanced at the equipment falling out of a nearby box. His mind flashed back to something he had seen in El Taco. Maybe there was a way of frightening the villains off.

What is Arthur's plan?

Tying Up Loose Ends

Bella Donna laughed as the flares whooshed over her head and lit up the sky behind her.

"What sort of bluff is that?" she sneered. "There are no Action Agents to see your signal."

"It wasn't an Agency signal," Arthur replied. "Look behind you."

Bella Donna spun around to see her men turn tail and head off into the distance. Her jaw dropped in amazement, as did her guns. This was the chance Arthur had been waiting for.

Arthur knotted a rope and threw it, right on target. As the lasso tightened around Bella Donna, Sleuth collected her guns. Just then Andrea and Zak appeared.

"That's the loose ends tied up," grinned Andrea. "Now we can contact base and clear our names."

But Arthur frowned. They still hadn't found the gold. Where was it? Then he remembered the equipment in the mine and smiled.

Where is the gold?

Clues

You will need to hold this page in front of a mirror to read the clues.

Pages 4-5
Look at the Action Code on page 3.

A =△ B = ∞

Pages 6-7
Look carefully at all the people in the pictures up to now. Do any faces reappear?

Pages 8-9
First decode the message on the piece of paper, then get rid of any extra letters.

Pages 10-11
A piece of tracing paper could be useful here.

Pages 12-13
Try swapping over some of the words then thinking back to front.

Pages 14-15
Try and fit all the pieces of the signpost together. Remember that you know where Arthur has come from.

Pages 16-17
Look for a safe route under the fence.

Pages 18-19
Try working from back to front, then swap the first letter of each word with the last.

Pages 20-21
Trace the fires back to the taps.

Pages 22-23
Look carefully for five spare parts scattered around.

Pages 24-25
Are there any familiar faces here? Does the train's name ring a bell?

Pages 26-27
Look for any objects that a cavalier wouldn't, or couldn't, wear.

Pages 28-29
Keep a sharp eye out for guards. You must avoid them at all cost.

Pages 30-31
Use Andrea's notes and the map to lead you there.

Pages 32-33
Look back to the mission log on page 13.

Pages 34-35
Follow Agent Zak's instructions exactly.

Pages 36-37
Has Bella Donna given Arthur anything that might be useful here?

Pages 38-39
Can you see anything lying around that they could use?

Pages 40-41
Look back to page 9. Can you see anything useful?

Page 42.
What was the equipment that they saw inside the mine? Have you seen any cacti growing somewhere that it shouldn't?

Answers

Pages 4-5

The message is written in Action Code. This is what it says when it is decoded:

> MEET CONTACT AGENT ANDREA
> AT STATUE OF IL DESPERADO. SHE
> WILL BE CARRYING A CRASH
> HELMET AND HAS VITAL
> INFORMATION. MAKE SURE YOU
> ARE NOT FOLLOWED.

Pages 6-7

These two men have been following Arthur through the town.

Look carefully at the pictures on pages 4-7 and you will see them.

Pages 8-9

This message has been written from back to front with the letter "o" inserted after every three letters. This is what it says when it is decoded:

> We are nearly ready, nothing must stop our operations. Follow Agent Arthur and dispose of him. Agent Andrea will be taken care of as planned.

Pages 10-11

Bella Donna and her cronies are heading for Avenida Rodeo.

Arthur knows that they started from the statue with the octagonal base.

By tracing the route from the tracking device and laying it over the street map, using the statue as a starting point, it is easy to work out where they have gone. The route is marked here in red.

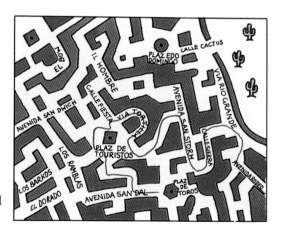

Pages 12-13

In coded message one, the second word has been swapped with the fourth, the sixth swapped with the eighth and so on. The message is then written back to front. Once decoded, and with punctuation added, it says:

> From desert base to El Taco from Bella Donna. We must move soon. I will arrive in El Taco on Saturday to take charge. We will leave town and proceed with Operation Smokescreen on the same day, then we will carry out Operation Sandstorm.

Coded message two is similar but here the first word is swapped with the fourth word and the fifth with the eighth. This message is also written back to front. Once decoded, and with punctuation added, it says:

> From desert base to Bella Donna in El Taco. All ready for your arrival here. We shall expect you once both operations have been completed. Good luck with Operation Smokescreen. Your target, the Pumperoilo Refinery, will be taken by surprise.

From the second message Arthur realizes that Bella Donna is heading for the Pumperoilo Refinery.

Pages 14-15

Arthur should head in this direction to reach the Pumperoilo Refinery.

He can work this out by piecing the signpost together. When he stands the signpost upright, with the arm marked El Taco pointing toward the road he has just come from, he can easily work out where each of the other roads lead to.

Pages 16-17

The safe route into the refinery is marked here.

Pages 18-19

This message is written from back to front then, starting with the last word, the first and last letter of each word is swapped around. When decoded it says:

To Bella Donna from double agent Arthur. We are carrying out our orders. The refinery will soon be destroyed but I am beginning to suspect double agent Andrea. Request permission to eliminate her.

Arthur remembers Bella Donna saying that the above message had been intercepted by the Action Agency. He looks at the fake ID cards he was given and puts two and two together . . . he and Agent Andrea have been set up to look like double agents who are working with the Spider Organization.

Pages 20-21

In order to stop the fires, Arthur should turn off the taps circled here.

The other taps feed oil into pipes that are not damaged.

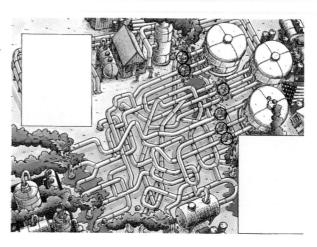

Pages 22-23

The six parts needed to complete the train are marked here with a cross.

Pages 24-25

Arthur recognizes the men as the ones who were following him earlier and knows that they belong to the Scorpion Mob.

He also notices that the train is called The Sandstorm Express. The fact that Bella Donna's men are aboard a train with this name makes Arthur certain that the train must have something to do with Operation Sandstorm.

Pages 26-27

Arthur has overlooked five things shown here.

He only has half a moustache.

How many cavaliers wore wrist watches?

Uncle Jake's tracking device is sticking out here.

He is wearing one normal boot.

His Action Agency Handbook is visible here.

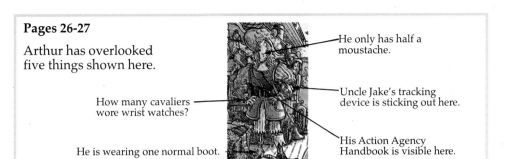

Pages 28-29

The safe route to the engine cab is marked in black.

Pages 30-31

The Action Agents boarded the Sandstorm Express at a junction where two lines meet. Starting with this information they work out the rest of their journey from Agent Andrea's notes. Heading directly out of the sun at dawn means that they must have started their journey heading due west. Andrea noticed the train was going at 40 mph. They were on the train for an hour and a half which means that they went about sixty miles. By using the scale on the map, they measure sixty miles along the tracks heading in a westerly direction. Using Arthur's information that they are due north of a rock formation, they can pinpoint their position.

The Action Agents are here.

They joined the train here.

The nearest oasis is here.

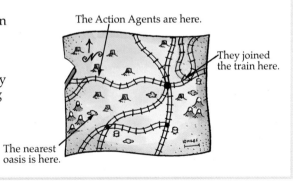

Pages 32-33

Agent Andrea remembers Agent Zak's last report in her mission log on page 13. It was from a ruined Alamo fort below Horseshoe Rock where Zak said he had left supplies. Agent Andrea looks around and sees a fort below a horseshoe-shaped rock. She hopes that this is where Agent Zak left his supplies.

Pages 34-35

The Action Agents follow Zak's instructions in his log and draw straight lines between the landmarks mentioned.

They form an arrow sign that points to the correct gorge. This is shown here.

Pages 36-37

Arthur is looking for the fake Scorpion Mob ID cards that Bella Donna gave him on pages 18-19 and which he put in his pocket.

They should convince the guard that Arthur and Andrea are members of the Scorpion Mob.

Pages 38-39

In order to trap the Scorpion Mobsters, the Action Agents must secure the doors that are the only way in or out of the barn.
They can do this by closing the doors then using the log, the ladder and the saw as bolts by placing them in the brackets.

Pages 40-41

Arthur remembers the Scorpion Mob signals from page 9. Two red flares indicates that there is danger and to retreat immediately. Arthur sees the flare gun and box of flares and knows that if he fires this signal, the Scorpion Mob in the distance will retreat.

Page 42

Arthur remembers the cactus shaped object that he found on page 14 and the ones that he saw on page 37, along with paint pots and a furnace. Putting two and two together, he realizes that the gold bars must have been heated up, then poured as liquid gold into the cactus shapes. They could then be painted to look like small cactus statuettes.

Racking his brains, he remembers where he has seen these statuettes before . . . Bella Donna was surrounded by them in her room in the bank on page 38. So this is where the gold is hidden.

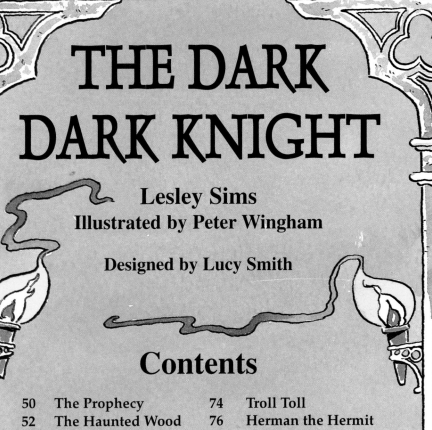

THE DARK DARK KNIGHT

Lesley Sims

Illustrated by Peter Wingham

Designed by Lucy Smith

Contents

The Prophecy

Welcome friend. I am Nerlym the Enchanter. The tale you are about to read began many centuries ago in a kingdom called Hamalot. Watch the story unfold in the smoke from my fire.

The kingdom of Hamalot was ruled by Good King Stan. It wasn't an easy job. King Stan had to spend most of his time fighting off fiendish beasts.

These beasts were servants of a villain known as the Dark Dark Knight. Tales of his wickedness were many but no one had ever seen him. He gave orders through an evil witch called Nastina.

Thurs 3pm:
Grand Battle
between
Good King Stan &
the Dark Dark
Knight!

Daily the Dark Dark Knight's powers grew stronger. Finally King Stan was challenged to a battle to decide the fate of the kingdom.

But just before the battle was due to begin, three of King Stan's most loyal knights vanished.

King Stan was captured, and held prisoner by an evil spell in Nastina's Tower of Desolation.

As the King was captured, milk curdled, toast burned and a violent storm began. Everyone waited in terror for the Dark Dark Knight to begin his reign.

Finally, the frightened people of Hamalot fled their towns and came to the castle to consult my Special Book of Knowledge.

Ye Special Book of Knowledge
Chapter 7 : Ye Prophecy

Lo there shall be a time when fear hangs a black cloud over ye land.

Then shall appear two saviours, St Halo and ye Martyr.

These Heroines shall descend from ye heavens seeking King Stan to save them from a darke, darke nighte.

Despite greate peril they shall undertake ye quest for King Stan.

But I must stop talking and let you find out what happened next. As the tale continues, maybe you can solve the puzzles and unravel the mystery of the Dark Dark Knight.

The people were very relieved.

The Haunted Wood

A thousand years after King Stan was captured, two friends called Haley and Martha were standing where the battle should have been fought . . . in Haley's kitchen.

They were taking a picnic to Yew Tree Wood. It had been growing wild for centuries and there were lots of creepy stories about it. Some even said the wood was haunted by ancient tree spirits.

Suddenly the radio crackled into life with a newsflash.

. . . very odd things have been happening. All the money in the town bank has turned to dough, the library books have become moths and the local museum has been ransacked. Now with the time at ten past nine we . . .

"Come on! Let's go or we'll miss the bus!" said Haley. Outside a fierce wind had sprung up from nowhere.

As they ran for the bus stop past the bank, a gust of wind blew a piece of paper straight into Haley's hand.

This is all my doing. Worse is to come until I find what I seek. You have been warned!

The Dark Dark Knight

On the bus she showed it to Martha. It was a note but it didn't seem to mean anything. They didn't even know who it was for, so Haley threw it away with her ticket. Just then the bus reached the wood and they jumped off, the odd note forgotten.

The wood was gloomier than normal as they hurried to their usual spot. But somehow, without noticing, they must have taken a wrong turn.

All of a sudden they were in a strange, unknown part of the wood, completely lost.

Then Martha spotted something behind a tangle of brambles. It was a door! Martha tried the handle but it was locked. A breeze rustled the leaves above her. "Key," they seemed to whisper.

Can you see a key?

53

Carved in Stone

Martha reached up for the key. But as she held it in her hand, the brambles parted as if by magic. Then slowly the door creaked open. Nervously they entered.

Inside was a chapel, eerily quiet. A stone tomb rose before them, bearing two lifelike figures of sleeping knights. A candle beside the tomb lit up a strange message on its base.

Haley tried to read it but it seemed to be in some ancient language. Then she realized it was in code and began to decipher the inscription.

She read it in amazement. Meanwhile Martha had found a horn hanging from a pillar. "WAIT!" Haley shouted. She was too late. Martha blew it.

What does the message say?

The Statues Awake

The walls began to shake and dust clouds filled the air. Martha and Haley watched in amazement as the two stone figures began to move.

They were stretching and sitting up. Haley and Martha stared in stunned silence.

The two stone knights, who weren't stone at all, stood up and brushed dust from their chainmail. The larger one glared at Martha. "Hey!" he said. "Where's the battle?"

"B-battle? W-what battle?" asked Martha in shock.

"The great one of course, against the villainous Dark Dark Knight," he said. The girls looked blank. "The whole of the kingdom's at stake," he added.

Then he noticed the inscription. "Hey Sir Roy, listen to this!" he said to the skinny knight, who was jumping around fighting a duel with the air.

"Treachery!" the skinny knight shouted. "What year is it then?" Haley answered automatically.

"Nineteen ninety what?" yelled the knight. "So who won the battle?" He paused and shuddered. "You don't suppose the Dark Dark Knight . . ?"

Haley and Martha didn't have a clue what was going on, but the Dark Dark Knight was the name on the note they'd thrown away in the bus.

"He must be stopped," said Sir Roy. "We have to get back to King Stan somehow. We MUST go to the castle!" he declared.

"There's no castle near here," said Martha, vaguely remembering a King Stan from her history book.

"Yes there is!" said Sir Roy and he began to describe the castle and its surrounding landmarks.

"Maybe there was a castle here once," said Haley, fishing a map from her bag and listening to the knight's description.

Where do you think the castle was?

It's a magnificent sight. A river runs to the east. Northeast are the famous Awlup Hills. A monastery lies directly to the south. It's just inside the City Walls. You must know it.

N

MAP OF STANTON
FREE
WITH EVERY BURGER!

STATION

AWLUP HILLS
HOSPITAL

BARON WAISTE
INDUSTRIES

TOWN
HALL

MUSEUM

CASTLE
CINEMA

BOATING
LAKE

TOWN
SQUARE

BULLFIELD
HOUSING ESTATE

SHOPPING
MALL

BURGER
BAR

POST
OFFICE

BANK

BUS
STATION

LEISURE
PARK WITH
MONSTER
MAZE

KEY

RAILWAY

RIVER

SITE OF RUIN

ANCIENT CITY WALL

MONKS
PARK

PITT
FOREST
SCHOOL

TOLL

BRIDGE

CASTLE
HOTEL

UNDERGROUND
CAR PARK

Hamalot's Burger Bar

Ten minutes later, they were at the site of the old castle, which was now Hamalot's Burger Bar (fast food with a medieval theme).

The knights were still with them and they weren't interested in hamburgers, they just wanted King Stan. All of a sudden a man came out of the kitchen. He was wearing a funny costume like the man behind the till.

But to the girls' surprise he raised his arms and greeted the knights like a long lost friend.

"Sir Roy! Sir Simon!" he cried. "What are you doing here?"

"Sir Percy?" exclaimed Sir Simon, the larger knight. He beamed at the man. "We've come to the castle but it seems to have gone."

He saw Martha and Haley's puzzled faces. "This is Sir Percy, the Knight Watchman and Keeper of Time," Sir Simon explained.

"Shh! I'm here undercover," Sir Percy said. "I wondered what had happened to you. Just after you vanished King Stan was captured," he told them. The knights gasped in disbelief. "You two must go back," he added.

"Use my Timedial," he said, giving Sir Roy a locket from his belt. "Say when and where you want to go, turn the pointer to the T factor and press the button. You can only go back, not forward and it will only work twice. I must go or I'll blow my cover."

Haley and Martha stared at him open-mouthed. Things were getting weirder by the minute.

The locket or Timedial turned out to be a pocket sundial, with instructions on the lid. Sir Roy read them quickly.

"Hamalot Castle, just after the battle," he gabbled, setting the pointer to three. He hit the button and the Timedial flew through the air. Haley caught it worriedly. She didn't think three was the answer.

Is three the right number?

To find the T factor:
Multiply the number of people going back by 6, if the number of people is 3 or less, or by 9 if the number is more than 3. Then subtract one third. If the answer is more than one digit, add them together until you have a single digit answer.

The Quest

There was a flash. Haley and Martha blinked. Hamalot's had gone. Instead they were in a blue room staring into the face of an old man with a long beard.

Behind them a man gave a shout. "The Heroines!" he said in awed tones and bowed. With a start the girls realized he meant them. Then the old man spoke.

"I am Nerlym the Enchanter," he said. "Welcome to Hamalot St. Halo and the Martyr."

"St. Halo and WHO?" said Martha. "I think you're confusing us with someone else!"

Nerlym shook his head. "We've been expecting you," he said. The girls were speechless.

"This is the Blue Briefing Room, inner sanctum of King Stan's loyal Knights of the Little Oval Table," Nerlym added. "We're planning your Quest to rescue King Stan."

The girls were horrified. Then Nerlym told them a tale of a dastardly knight and how only King Stan could defeat him.

After his story three things were clear. They'd gone back in time. They had to go on some quest – alone. Worst of all they couldn't go home until they had.

"This is about the Quest but in ancient Chivalric I'm afraid," said Nerlym, unfurling a scroll. It looked like an easy code. **Can you decipher the message?**

A Broken Sword

Nerlym gave them the scroll and led them outside. "Good luck!" he said. "By the way, Nastina only has power over three things. Anything else is illusion."

"What three things?" said Haley but Nerlym had gone. They were left, puzzled and alone, and all they had to go on was a confusing rhyme on a scroll.

Martha shrugged. "I suppose we'd better find shields and this chainmail," she said. "But where from?" The only person in sight was a gardener who seemed to be weeding. Perhaps he could help.

To their surprise, he was nibbling leaves. "You need Sir John, the swordsmith. Seee Sirrrr Johhhhn," he bleated.

He shook his head and his hair stood up in two pointed tufts. Were they imagining things? Could he be growing horns?

Martha and Haley stared in horror. He was definitely changing shape! As they stood bemused, he butted Haley onto a different path.

"A goat?!" she said to Martha spinning around. There in front of them was a hut. "Er, we need Sir John," she called to a knight in the doorway.

"That's me!" he said.

"The, er, gardener told us to see you," said Martha.

"Barry the Weregoat?" said Sir John. "He's harmless. Come in!"

Sir John found them tunics and two shields with cryptic messages he couldn't explain.

"Now, swords," said Sir John. "They're handmade and there's a six-week waiting list." He pointed to a heap of old metal on the floor. "You could look there."

"We can't make a sword out of pieces like a jigsaw!" said Martha.

"You might," Sir John grinned. **Which of the sword pieces fit together to make one sword?**

Follow that Monk!

Sir John smiled as the last piece of sword was put in place. To the girls' surprise it glowed and sprang together like new.

"Now we need to find these wise monks," said Martha, reading the scroll and as luck would have it, there outside the hut were two.

Martha grinned. "We can follow them," she said to Haley as the monks set off. "This Quest isn't so hard after all!"

They walked on and on until it felt like they'd been walking forever. But at last they arrived at the monastery.

"We're on a Quest to rescue King Stan," said Haley showing a monk the scroll. "We've come to ask what to do next."

First pass the entrance test!

A Little Knowledge is a Dangerous Thing! How Much do you Know? Enough to be Let in?

He sent them to the library where they were stopped by a second monk who pointed to a sign over the door.

"A test? This is like school," said Martha. The monk frowned and gave Haley a piece of parchment and an inky quill.

As Haley studied the parchment, Martha read the questions over her shoulder. "This is just like a puzzle book," Haley groaned.
Can you solve the quiz?

BROTHER BEN'S BRAINTEASERS

1. Fill in the missing values

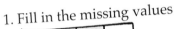

			39
			?
			?
25	?	31	?

2. Add the bell and candle

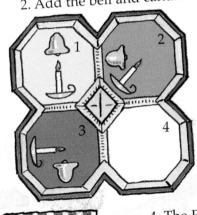

3. Find the Fiends!

D	W	B	H	A	G	I	L
E	R	E	T	S	N	O	M
R	D	A	F	R	T	G	F
I	W	S	G	N	O	R	T
P	A	T	A	O	A	L	C
M	R	I	G	W	N	V	L
A	G	R	D	F	H	A	B
V	E	R	T	C	E	P	S

Can you strike out all ten fiends hidden in the grid? (They are listed around the edge of the parchment.)

4. The Pilgrims' Progress

Two pilgrims set out from shrines in nearby towns. Each is visiting the shrine the other has just left. They travel at exactly the same speed, yet one takes 1 hour and 20 minutes to arrive, while the other reaches his shrine in only 80 minutes. How?

MONSTER GIANT OGRE DWARF

HAG BEAST VAMPIRE DRAGON

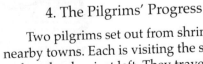

SPECTRE   TROLL

Books and Clues

With a stern "Be quiet in there," they were let in. Inside sat row upon row of hooded figures, all bent over high desks. Each was painstakingly copying a manuscript. A monk came up to Martha.

"We're on a quest," she said. "We need to know how to get to Nastina's Tower." Haley rustled the scroll. "Ssshhh!" came a dozen voices from behind.

The monk glanced at the scroll and disappeared. Soon he was back with an old book called Tall Tales, stuffed full of papers and dried flowers.

A jumble of papers? How would they help? Haley felt confused. Then she realized that if they pieced together all the information from the papers and put it into the right order, they would know what to do next.

Where should they go first?

Brother Gregory's Alphabet Chant

An exercise to warm up the voice

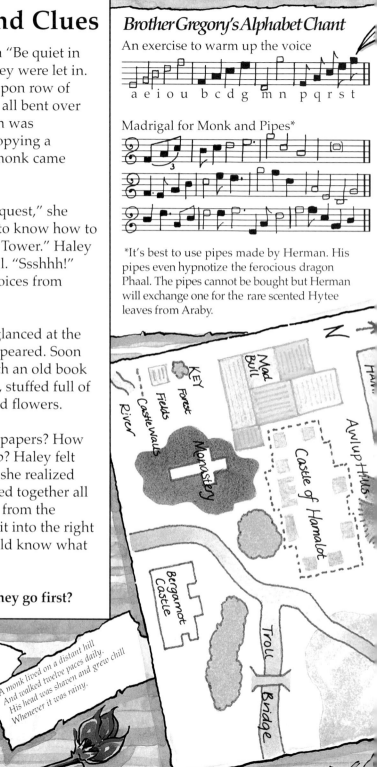

a e i o u b c d g m n p q r s t

Madrigal for Monk and Pipes*

*It's best to use pipes made by Herman. His pipes even hypnotize the ferocious dragon Phaal. The pipes cannot be bought but Herman will exchange one for the rare scented Hytee leaves from Araby.

A monk sat on the cloister steps.
A wind blew from the East.
"I'll have to go," he sadly said,
"I've missed the winter feast."

A monk lived on a distant hill
And walked twelve paces daily.
His head was shaven and grew chill
Whenever it was rainy.

KING KIDNAPPED!

by Brother Dan

Good King Stan has been the victim of a terrible trick and is now held prisoner in the grim Tower of Desolation.

As the Great Battle against the Dark Dark Knight was about to begin, three loyal KLOTs were spirited away and King Stan was grabbed by Nastina's Nasties.

Each day King Stan is away, the power of the Dark Dark Knight grows stronger. Any day now he will arrive to take control.

Learn to read & write in 5 days! For further details write to The Monastery.

EARL GREY OF BERGAMOT CASTLE:

importer of the finest spices and leaves from Araby.

GRAND FAYRE

This was a huge success with a record crowd of 57, two pigs and a goat. The winner of the Beautiful Turnip competition was Nag Miggins. Well done Nag!

The Wandring Minstrels

at the village inn.
Doors open at 4pm.

Monastery Rhymes
A funky monk picked up his lute
And sang a little song.
Ten other monks threw rotten fruit
Each note he plucked was wrong.

To release a knight from evil enchantment call his name three times.

Tall Tales: The Towers of Hamalot

The Tower of Desolation

The Tower of Desolation lies in the middle of the Barren Wastes and is home to the evil Nastina.

Though there is no doubt it exists, no one has a clear idea of what it looks like because it is usually invisible.

The Tower is defended by three ingenious but invisible obstacles. Each one must be overcome before the next one will appear.

The door to the Tower is blocked by Silverkeys the Guardian. He is protected by Three Crones who in turn are guarded by the dragon Phaal.

Phaal and the three crones

Phaal lives in a devious labyrinth. Though immortal, he can be hypnotized. Until he's defeated, the exit to the Crones is hidden.

An artist's impression of the Tower of Desolation

In Deep Trouble

First they had to visit Earl Grey for Hytee leaves. It wasn't far to go but it was getting dark, so the monks invited them to stay.

At sunrise they set off. Soon they were on the edge of a great forest. But before long Martha was moaning. Her feet hurt.

"What we need is a horse," she said. No sooner than she had spoken, and to her immense surprise, a horse appeared from behind some trees.

"This is weird!" cried Martha leaping astride the horse. It swung around and charged back into the forest. Haley just managed to jump on as Martha shot past.

A terrifying ten-minute ride followed. They clung to the horse's mane as it galloped over bushes, under branches and around trees at high speed. Then it stopped – so abruptly that the girls flew over its head into a deep pit.

"Gotcha!" bellowed a voice. Martha and Haley looked up to see a hideous creature above them.

"Ha! New servants for me cookings and me cleanings," it said. "Stay there till I needs you."

Haley and Martha climbed to their feet, relieved to find they had no broken bones.

"What next?" said Haley crossly, looking at the leering creature. "He looks like he's escaped from a fairy tale."

Martha didn't hear. She'd seen a stone slab propped against the pit wall with three sentences on it. She read the first one out.

"Ha! Them's me riddles," said the creature. "If you gets them right I might let you go . . ."

Martha grinned. "They're just anagrams. That's easy!" she said and reeled off the answers.

". . . then again I might not," the creature added grumpily.

"I wish I'd never jumped on that horse," said Martha.

When Haley fell she'd landed on something hard in her pocket. She felt it curiously. "That's it!" she cried. "We can easily get out!"

I GAIN MAC spells *Abracadabra*

WORDS to fight *a duel*

EVEN RAT DU have a *daring fun time*

What is Haley's escape plan?

Arabian Knights

In a flash they were back on the edge of the forest. This time they ignored the horse and ran on. Half an hour later they reached a river. Earl Grey's castle stood on the opposite bank.

Some time later, they squelched up a long drive, under a vast gateway and in through the main doors.

Prince Coriander, who doesn't wear yellow, brought gems.

The knight wearing blue came by elephant.

Neither Sir Nutmeg nor the knight in green came by elephant.

They had stepped straight into a Great Hall. There were tables full of magnificent food but it was all growing cold. To their surprise a round, fat man smiled as they entered.

"Welcome!" he cried. "At last we can eat. Name your challenge strangers!" Martha and Haley were puzzled.

"It's an old rule," said the man. "We can't begin our feast until a puzzle or problem has been solved. How can we help? Are you damsels in distress?"

"Not really," said Haley. "We need Hytee leaves from Araby."

"Ha!" cried the man. "Then I shall set you a puzzle. The four royal knights on my right are from Araby. But which one has the Hytee leaves? If you can't guess you'll be sent to the dungeons for a year and a day."

To Martha and Haley's relief, hungry guests shouted clues. Soon they could identify each knight, say what he had brought and how he'd arrived.

Which knight has the Hytee leaves?

Underground Secrets

They were given a tiny packet, which Haley put in her pocket, and they set out again. The landscape grew bleak. After a while they reached a fork in the track. "Which way now?" said Martha. "This wasn't on the map."

"Look, we can ask him!" said Haley, pointing to a figure in the distance. But something about the way he approached, bent over and hurrying, made them hesitate.

As he passed they saw his crest – the same as the one on the note. Was he one of the Dark Dark Knight's men? They had to find out.

A pair of giant rocks loomed ahead. The man slipped between them and vanished. Silently, they followed him.

They climbed down some steps and found themselves in a passageway. The man was in a brightly-lit chamber.

They hid by the doorway and watched him. He was reading a letter. Then he tore it up, threw it on the fire and hurried to the doorway.

Haley and Martha dashed back up the stairs around a corner and held their breath. To their huge relief, the man rushed off in the opposite direction. They waited for a few seconds and then ran into the room.

Martha quickly snatched up a poker to retrieve the fragments of letter. Luckily they had fallen onto the grate and the fire had hardly touched them.

Haley looked at one of the fragments and gasped. "It's from the Dark Dark Knight!" she said. "If we can put it back together, we might learn more about him!"

What does the letter say?

Dark Dark Knight
Yours hurriedly,

Boy with them). Go straight to those drafted Heroines have turned away. I called the battle too soon. Goblet must be used on All me and my reign will last a flashing box. When I have future. But I have found it! I its Nerhym's father. He feared

Goblet is a legend. I have proof invincible. Those foolish XLOTS moon's reflection in it, shall be he who uses it to drink water legend of the Moon Goblet. I have spent many years memorize this letter, then patient. The time has come to a week ago. When will I return I expect you are wondering To my faithful page, Fred —

where I've been since the battle to claim my throne? Soon. Be reveal my masterplan. Read and DESTROY IT! studying the This says that with the immortal and think the it exists!

It was made in the time of power and threw it far into the even took a picture of it with drunk from it no one will stop forever! I made one error. The Ghouls' Eve, still a few days Now time is short. Already up (and brought Simon and Nastina and tell her.

The

Troll Toll

It was hard to imagine how much power the Dark Dark Knight would wield if his plan succeeded. But they knew one thing. He had to be stopped. Haley ran to the steps.

"Wait!" said Martha pulling her back. "That man was going to Nastina's tower too. We'll be quicker if we follow him."

The steps led to a tunnel. Martha scrambled along. Haley followed, noticing some paper on the ground. Martha must have dropped it in her haste, she thought and pocketed it.

Past the tunnel, the way ahead was blocked by a river. They were about to cross the bridge when something jumped out at them.

"This is a troll toll bridge," it said. "I'm the troll! You have to pay me a toll before you cross."

"If you can't pay, you'll have to fight my knight," it added and gave a piercing whistle.

A strange-looking knight appeared before them. He was huge and silent and his eyes were glazed over, as if he wasn't seeing anything. He didn't react to them at all, just walked slowly and silently in their direction.

He grasped Haley's shoulder and led her to a horse. She tried to wriggle free but his grip was unshakable. Then he gave her a lance. He seemed oblivious to the fact that she was half his size and not even a knight.

Martha watched in horror. There was no way Haley could win. Something else about the knight bothered Martha, apart from the fact that he was in league with a horrible warty troll.

As the knight mounted his horse, Martha recognized his coat of arms. Of course! He was a KLOT. But how could she stop him? Then it dawned on her – he'd been enchanted. She'd read in the library that to call his name three times would break the spell. But what was his name?

Do you know?

Herman the Hermit

Martha called his name and Sir Gavin awoke. The girls raced across the bridge chased by the troll. Sir Gavin raced after the troll and chased it away.

As they left the bridge, a mist came from nowhere. It wrapped itself around Martha and Haley until they couldn't see each other.

Ow! Watch the sword Haley!

Oops!

Martha? That didn't sound like you. Wh-who's there? I warn you, I'm armed!

"Only me!" said a voice unhelpfully. "I was divining."

The mist began to lift and they saw the owner of the voice.

"I'm Herman," he grinned and gave a little bow.

It was Herman the Hermit, the maker of pipes. Haley told him about their quest. The leaves were very crushed but Herman didn't seem to mind. "Hytee leaves for me? Splendid!" he said.

His hut was cramped and smelled damp. He hunted for the pipe, chattering to himself. "Visitors! Makes a change. I don't see anyone now Nastina's next door. Who wants to be near her?"

"Even if her Tower's invisible," he went on. "That's just her tricksy magic that is. You only see it when you break through the other obstacles. Aha!" he cried at last, waving a pipe and some music.

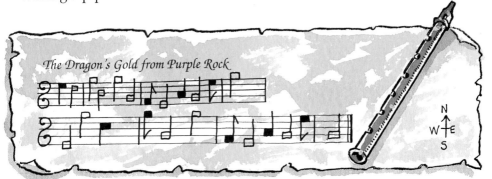

The Dragon's Gold from Purple Rock

"The problem," he added, "is that my pipes only hypnotize the dragon if you can find him. I've spent years hunting, even bought music from a door-to-door minstrel who promised it would lead me to him. But I sat on the Purple Rock and played it. Nothing happened."

"Suppose it's not music at all," said Haley slowly, studying it. She'd seen some like it recently. "I think it's coded directions made to look like music. The Purple Rock is where we start from."

Where should they go?

The Labyrinth

By a red rock Haley took out the pipe and blew it. Nothing happened. Meanwhile Martha was excitedly reading two pieces of paper which had fallen out of Haley's pocket.

"You dropped them," Haley said. But they weren't Martha's.

Fred,
You must feed Phaal. If I leave the Tower, my hold over Stan is weakened. Go to the Red Rock and say, "Mighty Nastina, she who commands serpents, stone and steel, now bids you answer her demand: the dragon's lair reveal!" You will find yourself where I have marked 'X' on this plan. Nastina

They were a note from Nastina and a plan of the labyrinth. Martha recited the rhyme on the note, then . . . did they sink or did the ground rise up? Suddenly they were in a high-walled tunnel, open to the sky. The only way out was to find the middle, for Phaal guarded the exit at the maze's heart.

What is the route to Phaal?

78

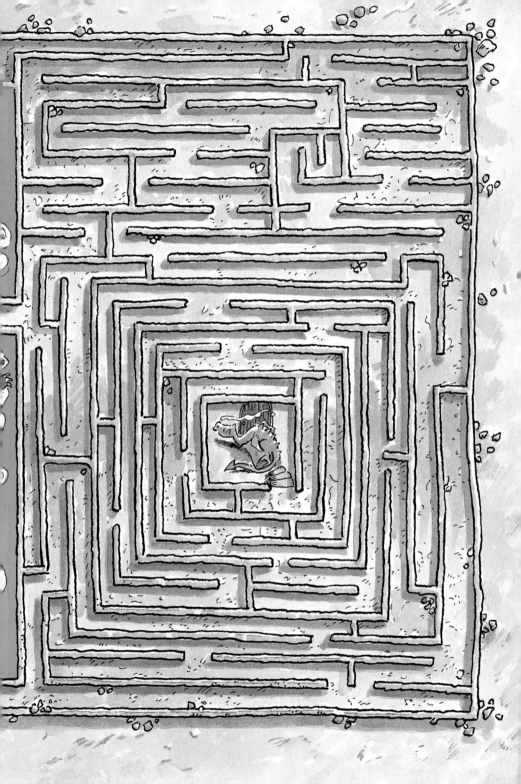

A Dragon and Three Crones

At last they reached the steps which led down to Phaal. The gaping mouth of a cave grew bigger and darker as they went closer. It glowed a deep red. Red? thought Haley. How odd.

"GET OUT! It's his mouth!" cried Martha. "Quick, the pipe!"

They leapt back as Phaal reared up before them. Haley's mouth felt dry but she stuck the pipe in and blew. A few quavery notes came out. They sounded terrible.

Phaal paused. Martha shut her eyes fearing the worst. But Haley played some more, slowly moving the pipe from side to side, like a snake charmer.

Phaal followed the pipe, from left to right to left. Slowly his eyes closed and he sank down onto his huge pile of treasure. A rumbling snore told them he was asleep.

Now they could see daylight coming into the labyrinth through three holes in the far wall.

Martha led the way over Phaal's treasure to the first exit. But an old woman blocked the way out.

"I cannot see to let you pass. Find my specs or stay stuck fast," she cackled.

At the second exit an even older, uglier hag stopped them.

"You want to leave? You'll have to shout. With my hearing trumpet I'd let you out," she bellowed.

At the last exit was the ugliest crone of all. "Wiffout my teef I cannot chew. If I faint from hunger, you won't get frew," she gabbled. "And only one of free won't do," she added cryptically.

Haley and Martha looked at her, puzzled. One of free? "Oh, three!" said Haley. "We have to find their three things to get out of here. We'd better find them fast before he wakes up," she added.

Martha looked at the sleeping dragon. "I hope they're not underneath him," she whispered.

Can you find the crones' missing things?

Guardian of the Tower

The three crones grasped their things and turned away, gloating. Haley and Martha slipped through the third exit.

Outside, they stopped and stared in amazement. Half shrouded in mists, a ghostly wall was growing before them.

A misty tower rose up behind the wall. Gradually, the mist took on a more solid look.

Then a door studded with spikes appeared. Haley touched it cautiously. It felt real enough. Gripping the sword, she opened the door and they went in.

They found themselves in a courtyard paved in black and white. A small man with several keys jangling on his belt came up to them.

"So you got past Phaal and his fair maidens," he said with an evil laugh. "You won't defeat me. There's only one route to the Tower. Step on the wrong stone at the wrong time and . . ."

He threw a twig onto a black square. The twig fizzed and then dissolved, running down between the cracks in the stones.

"Only the white squares with flags are always safe," he said. He pointed to a sundial. "If you reach the door before twelve, I'll unlock it. If not, and you're still alive, you'll be left to rot in the dungeons."

Martha gulped. The shadow was almost at twelve now. What could they do? Then a line from the scroll ran through her mind.

Your shields help to cross her floor. Martha studied the shields. "That's it!" she said. "The lines on your shield show which way we go, north, south, east or west. The symbols on my shield show how many squares we cross each time. I have two green trees, so whenever you have a green line, we cross two squares. Your first line is green and points north, so we go two squares north. Follow me!"
Can you find a route to the door?

Inside the Tower

The tower door slammed shut behind them. "You won't find it so easy to get out," snarled the man from outside.

Haley and Martha looked around. They were in a small, dimly-lit hallway which was almost filled by a spiral staircase.

Martha took a deep breath and started to climb. Warily, Haley followed her.

Darkened rooms led off the stairs. The girls peered around half-closed doors, each time terrified that one would open on Nastina, evil mistress of the tower.

Finally they found a brightly decorated room. A smiling knight called to them. Was this King Stan?

Haley felt uneasy. The figure didn't seem real. Martha was going in when Haley held her back. "Wait!" she said.

As she spoke, the knight and the room vanished. They were left teetering on the brink of a gaping hole. Haley hauled Martha back from the edge just in time.

Terrified, they climbed higher, finally reaching the top of the tower. A dazed knight was slumped in the corner of a room at the end of the staircase.

He didn't even look up as they came in. "King Stan?" said Haley. The knight groaned. "Help me get him up," Haley said to Martha. "We must get him out of here."

"I don't think so," said a rasping voice behind them. Nastina stood in the doorway, her arms raised above her head, lightning flashing from her fingers.

She entered and the doorway vanished. Thunderbolts shook the room as four new doorways sprang up. Each revealed a deadly trap.

"Exits of spider, serpents, stone and steel," laughed Nastina. "But dare you use them? You can only go through one anyway," she said and vanished.

Haley frowned. Suddenly she remembered Nerlym's last words to them. Then she thought of the rhyme that made the labyrinth appear. She smiled. One doorway was safe.

Which one is it?

A Call to Arms

As soon as Haley stepped into the web, it vanished. They dragged the dopey King down the spiral staircase. Once outside, he quickly revived.

"Into battle!" he cried and then stopped. "Where am I? Who are you? What's going on?" he asked.

"No time to explain," Martha panted. "We must go to Hamalot now. I hope we're not too late."

"We'll be there in a trice!" said King Stan, clicking his fingers. "To Hamalot!" he cried. And quicker than a blink they were there.

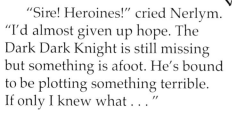

"Sire! Heroines!" cried Nerlym. "I'd almost given up hope. The Dark Dark Knight is still missing but something is afoot. He's bound to be plotting something terrible. If only I knew what . . . "

"He wants to be invincible," said Martha. "He's after some goblet and I think he's found it." Nerlym gasped. "I'm sure I've seen it somewhere," Martha muttered to herself. "But where?"

"We must find it first," King Stan declared. "Call my KLOTs. Tell them to prepare for battle!"

"They're all over the castle," said Nerlym. "It will take me all afternoon to find them. But I won't mention a battle or they won't come. I'll just say the king is free!"

Nerlym hurried away. The knights were enjoying a free afternoon but finally nearly everyone was gathered in the Hall.

"The Dark Dark Knight will threaten us no more!" King Stan declared. The knights cheered. "We leave now for the final battle!" he added. The knights began to make excuses.

"We shall all leave now for . . . er, where are we going?" said King Stan. In a flash Martha remembered where she'd seen the goblet before.

Do you?

The Last Battle of All

King Stan clicked his fingers. Instantly the castle became the burger bar but the goblet had gone. Outside Haley saw a dark figure by the water fountain.

Everyone ran to the fountain. A knight in black was watching the moon's reflection on the water's surface. With a triumphant cry he scooped up the reflection.

"STOP!" cried King Stan rushing up to him and knocking the goblet from the knight's hand.

A desperate duel began. At first the knights cheered but they soon fell silent.

The Dark Dark Knight was winning. He flicked King Stan's sword from his hand.

Look, the sword's gone through his mask!

That's got him! Scratch his face!

Haley quickly handed King Stan her sword. Sparks flashed like stars as it left the scabbard. Slowly the tables were turned.

At last the Dark Dark Knight was pinned against the fountain, the sword at his throat. King Stan was about to unmask him when . . .

. . . clouds of black smoke surrounded them, leaving everyone choking. When the smoke cleared the Dark Dark Knight had gone.

The knights looked at each other in dismay. "The villain has escaped!" said King Stan in horror. Haley and Martha looked around. He was no longer the Dark Dark Knight but he hadn't gone far. They knew where he was.

Do you?

A Dark Knight Ends

"It's him!" cried Haley, pointing. King Stan refused to believe her. It couldn't be one of his KLOTs.

"We can prove it!" said Martha. "The Dark Dark Knight wrote a letter to his servant Fred telling him all about us. Only Nerlym and the KLOTs knew we'd arrived."

How dare you accuse ME, Sir Jack Upall!

"When we left Hamalot castle there was one knight missing," Haley added. "But now all the KLOTs are here. If you want any more proof, look at his cheek. It was grazed in the duel."

King Stan told the knight to remove his hood. There on his cheek was a trickle of dried blood. "Grab him!" ordered King Stan.

He turned to Haley and Martha. "Thank you for all your help. Now we must return to our own time before any more harm is done."

He clicked his fingers, there was a flash and then King Stan, his knights and Nerlym had gone. Haley and Martha were alone.

"Let's go home," Martha said after a few seconds. "I want to check my old history book. Do you think it describes King Stan and his glorious rescue by Saint Halo and the Martyr?"

Clues

Pages 52-53
Keys don't grow on trees . . . do they?

Pages 54-55
Each word has been reversed and an extra letter added in front. The extra letters also hide a message.

Pages 56-57
Some landmarks may have changed over the centuries.

Pages 58-59
Sir Roy used 9 in his sum, yet only he and Sir Simon were going back.

Pages 60-61
Chivalric breaks up words into groups of four and adds three letters to all words not ending in a vowel.

Pages 62-63
Fit the pieces of sword together. There are pieces for more than one sword.

Pages 64-65
1. Find the value of the jug first.
2. The bell and candle move around in a sequence.
3. Read up, down, diagonally and from side to side.
4. How many minutes in 1 hour, 20 minutes?

Pages 66-67
Start with the Tower of Desolation and work back.

Pages 68-69
Solving the anagrams didn't help Martha, but something she said has given Haley an idea.

Pages 70-71
Using what you know you can fill in the gaps. As Coriander didn't ride the camel or horse he must have come by elephant or mule. But he brought gems and the mule carried wooden things. So Coriander rode the elephant and is the knight in blue.

Pages 72-73
Trace the pieces and fit them together.

Pages 74-75
A KLOT was missing when they arrived. Check the shields on page 60.

Pages 76-77
The alphabet chant in the library gives each note a letter.

Pages 78-79
Watch out for blind alleys.

Pages 80-81
Search the treasure carefully.

Pages 82-83
A red line means one square, a green line means two squares and a blue line means three squares.

Pages 84-85
The rhyme tells you which three things Nastina has power over.

Pages 86-87
Martha must have seen the Moon Goblet before they went back in time.

Pages 88-89
The Dark Dark Knight has gone but another knight has arrived. Who is he?

Answers

Pages 52-53

The key is circled below.

Pages 54-55

Each word has been written back to front and begins with an extra letter. With the letters in the right order, the inscription reads:

Here lie two most puny knights, the KLOTs Sir Simon and Sir Roy. I cast a spell on these two knights and transported them here in a deep sleep. In this chapel they shall sleep forever, unless someone is clever enough to decipher this message and wake them. The Horn of Awakening will rouse them. Blow it if you dare . . .   Nastina AD995

The extra letters also make a sentence: Don't meddle with things you don't understand. You will live to regret it! N

Pages 56-57

If you match the descriptions of the old landmarks to the places shown on the modern map, you will see that Hamalot's Burger Bar stands on the site of Stan's castle. The three hills are now the Awlup Hills Hospital.

Pages 58-59

The right number was 8. Sir Roy should have multiplied 2 (him and Sir Simon) by 6. Instead he multiplied 2 by 9 = 18, less a third = 12 and then added 2 and 1 together.

3 was completely wrong. It's surprising the Timedial worked at all. Perhaps someone was watching to help the Prophecy come true.

Pages 60-61

Chivalric breaks up words into groups of four and adds "ric" to the end of every group not finishing with a vowel. Decoded the scroll reads:

The Quest for King Stan

St. Halo, Martyr,
this your Quest:
To free Nastina's captured guest.
First you must find two
chainmail vests,
A starry sword and shields.
Then seek wise monks
who'll tell you more
Of how to reach Nastina's door.
Your shields will help
to cross her floor
And then her fate is sealed.

Pages 62-63

The pieces they need have been circled.

The sword fits together like this:

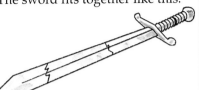

Pages 64-65

1. Missing values

 A jug of apple juice is 13

 An apple is 5

A chunk of cheese is 7

2. Bell and candle

4. Pilgrims' Progress

One hour 20 minutes is the same as 80 minutes.

3. Find the Fiends

D	W	B	H	A	G	I	L
E	R	E	T	S	N	O	M
R	D	A	F	R	D	G	P
I	W	S	G	N	O	R	T
P	A	T	A	O	A	L	C
M	R	I	G	W	N	V	L
A	G	R	D	F	H	A	B
V	E	R	T	C	E	P	S

Pages 66-67

To enter the Tower of Desolation Haley and Martha must first defeat Silverkeys the Guardian of the Tower. They learn this from the book "Tall Tales." The book also tells them that to reach Silverkeys, they must get past the Three Crones – who can't be reached without finding and defeating Phaal the dragon.

The sheet of music tells them that Phaal can be hypnotized with one of Herman's pipes and that he will swap a pipe for Hytee leaves from Araby.

An advertisement in the newspaper says that Earl Grey imports spices and leaves from Araby, so Bergamot Castle is where they should start.

Pages 68-69

Haley still has Sir Percy's Timedial. Her plan is to go back in time to just before they saw the horse and then ignore it.

(The three anagrams are magician, sword and adventure.)

Pages 70-71

Duke Turmeric who wears red and rode a camel, brought the Hytee leaves.

Prince Coriander wears blue, came by elephant and brought gems.

Sir Nutmeg wears yellow and rode a mule carrying the carved wooden things.

Lord Fenugreek wears green, rode a horse and brought perfume.

Pages 72-73

When the letter is pieced together, this is what it says:

To my faithful page, Fred –

    I expect you are wondering where I've been since the battle a week ago. When will I return to claim my throne? Soon. Be patient. The time has come to reveal my masterplan. Read and memorize this letter, then *DESTROY IT!*

    I have spent many years studying the legend of the Moon Goblet. This says that he who uses it to drink water with the moon's reflection in it, shall be immortal and invincible. Those foolish KLOTs think the Goblet is a legend. I have proof it exists!

    It was made in the time of Nerlym's father. He feared its power and threw it far into the future. But I have found it! I even took a picture of it with a flashing box. When I have drunk from it no one will stop me and my reign will last forever! I made one error. The Goblet <u>must</u> be used on All Ghouls' Eve, still a few days away. I called the battle too soon. Now time is short. Already those dratted Heroines have turned up (and brought Simon and Roy with them). Go straight to Nastina and tell her.

              Yours hurriedly,
            The Dark Dark Knight

Pages 74-75

He is Sir Gavin Goode. He was enchanted by Nastina at the same time as Sir Simon and Sir Roy, and given to the troll.

Pages 76-77

The music can be translated using Brother Gregory's Alphabet Chant shown in the library on pages 66-67.

If you match the notes from there with the ones on Herman's music, a message is revealed:

Go nine paces N(orth) and ten paces E(ast).

Pages 78-79

Their route through the labyrinth is shown in red.

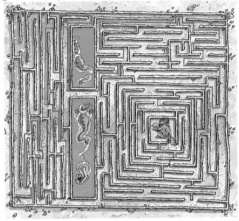

Pages 80-81

The three missing things have been circled.

Pages 82-83

This is their route across the courtyard.

Pages 84-85

The spider doorway is the exit they must take.

Nerlym told Martha and Haley on page 62 that Nastina only had power over three things.

The rhyme to make the labyrinth appear (page 78) tells you what the three things are: serpents, stone and steel. Three of the doorways show serpents, steel spikes and crumbling stone steps.

Nerlym said anything else was an illusion, so Haley realizes that the spider and his web are not really there.

Pages 86-87

The Moon Goblet is here, in Hamalot's Burger Bar, being used to hold straws.

Pages 88-89

The Dark Dark Knight has been circled. He's Sir Jack Upall, who has just appeared from nowhere.

He was seen on the very first page when Haley and Martha arrived in Hamalot Castle. But he hasn't been seen since.

When Nerlym went around the castle collecting knights, he was the only knight who wasn't there.

Finally, there was one other clue to the Dark Dark Knight's identity. Haley and Martha didn't mention it. Did you spot it?

THE CRIMEBUSTERS INVESTIGATE

Mark Fowler

Illustrated by Ann Johns

Designed by Lucy Parris
Edited by Corinne Stockley

Contents

About this book

The Crimebusters Investigate is an exciting tale of mystery and detection. Throughout the book, you are plunged into tricky puzzles which you must solve to make sense of the story. There are clues to help you on page 139, and you can check all the answers on pages 140 to 144.

A Summer Job

Kaz Smiley was not having a good summer. Somehow or other, she'd agreed to work mornings at Grimebusters, her Aunt Mary's cleaning business.

"The extra money's great," she told her friend Matt, "but I can think of at least five hundred things I'd rather be doing this summer!"

One hot, sticky Wednesday, Kaz drifted into the Grimebusters office, hoping that for once there wouldn't be too many jobs lined up for her. She pulled a note from the notice board…

…and then wished she hadn't. It looked like today was going to be a *bad* day.

If there's dirty work around call
GRIMEBUSTERS
Quick and efficient service
234 - 487 - 34

Wed August 4
Dear Kaz,
Called away on urgent personal business. Back next week. Busy morning for you, I'm afraid!
1. Scrub houseboat Aurora at Orlando Wharf until shipshape.
2. Shampoo Mrs. Turnbull's carpets with Wandascrub Suds.
3. Sweep chimneys at 124 Wharf Road.
4. Deliver leaflets from box 5.
Please lock up carefully.
Aunt Mary

Grimebuster!

Kaz gulped and read the note again. If she got all that done in one morning it really *would* be a miracle. Still, at least then she could have a couple of days off.

Watch out! Every single leaflet that we delivered in July had a misprint! DO NOT deliver any more leaflets from box 4. Mary

Weighed down by buckets, mops, brooms, vacuum cleaners and assorted bottles, Kaz staggered out to the van and set off for Orlando Wharf.

When she arrived, she spotted the Aurora at once...

...and got to work.

First she scrubbed the portholes...

...then she swabbed the decks...

...and polished the ship's wheel.

At last the houseboat was clean, but there were two more calls to make…

…and a whole box of leaflets to deliver.

WANTED

Amazingly, Kaz made it back to the Grimebusters office by 12:20 – with ten minutes to spare before the end of her morning.

Exhausted, she collapsed onto a pile of old boxes for a quick snooze. But a few minutes later, her peace was shattered…

IF THERE'S DIRTY WORK AROUND CALL
CRIMEBUSTERS
234 487 94
31 BACK STREET

Marvello Mansion

I need your help... a terrible mess... please come right away – Marvello Mansion, Morello Road...

Prrrring! The Grimebusters telephone began to ring. As soon as Kaz answered, a shrill, ear-piercing voice launched into a long speech, summoning her to a place called Marvello Mansion.

It all sounded very dramatic, but could a cleaning job really be *that* urgent?

Well – only one way to find out, thought Kaz. She grabbed a city map and set off. Half an hour and six wrong turns later, she finally found Morello Road. It was in a part of Allegro she had never been to before.

Marvello Mansion certainly looked like a real mansion. Nervously, Kaz swallowed hard and started up the path toward the marble doorway.

Before she got there, the door was flung open by a large, well-dressed woman. She seemed very flustered, and also a bit surprised.

"You're a lot younger than I'd expected," she said in her shrill voice. "But I'm sure you know your job. I'm Constanza Smith – the opera singer," she added. "No doubt you've heard of me."

And with these words, she pushed Kaz through the door.

Constanza led Kaz into a large drawing room where a strange collection of people crowded around her, all jabbering at once, and very loudly. The room was a total mess, but no one even *mentioned* cleaning.

As she listened, Kaz got more and more confused, but then she remembered Aunt Mary's note on the office door. Maybe she hadn't been called in as a cleaner at all.

What do you think?

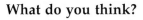

103

^CGrimebusters!

You simply *must* find it for me. I couldn't *possibly* call in the police.

Matt? I'm not a cleaner any more – I'm a detective! And I'm going to need your help...

These people thought Kaz was a detective – a Crimebuster, not a Grimebuster! And they wanted her to find a stolen medallion, the Traitor's Knot.

Kaz opened her mouth to explain the mistake. But then she stopped. Being a detective would be much more exciting than cleaning carpets, she thought. She'd need some help ...her friend Matt, of course! Trying to sound like a pro, she turned to Constanza.

"This case might be tricky," she said. "I think I'll need to call in my partner."

Alone in a side room, she rang Matt's number, then launched into a hurried explanation. Matt agreed to help at once.

Twenty minutes later, he was outside Marvello Mansion, armed with a notebook and trying to look the part. Kaz let him in, and the two detectives had a rapid 'private conference'.

Right, first we ask them all questions...

What kind of questions?

Well... er... about what happened, of course.

104

But when Constanza bustled back into the hall a few minutes later, she told them that her four guests had all left.

"Oh dear," whispered Kaz to Matt. "Not a very good start. Still, we'll just have to catch up with them later. What next?"

"Comb the scene of the crime for clues," pronounced Matt confidently.

This was all very well if you knew what you were looking for. There were all kinds of things on the floor, including some scraps from the display case and an overturned wastebasket, but nothing looked particularly promising.

Finally, though, some torn-up scraps of paper did catch Kaz's attention. Once pieced together, they revealed an interesting message.

What does it say?

Ne
devel
you pla
yet? Meet
morning at
make arran
for the ha
be at the
end

Wednesday 4th
...ed to discuss latest
...ments. Ha...
...nned f...
me

ve
had swoop
tomorrow
ten to
...ments I'll
the

of
your road.
please be
prompt.

...café at
...over

THE TRAITOR'S KNOT
MEDALLION

Historic piece, thought to have once belonged
to Roger de Fey, governor of Allegro and opera patron.

On The Case

Was the torn note a clue? Kaz stuffed the pieces in her pocket, just in case. Meanwhile Matt had decided their next move. "We must figure out who the suspects are," he said.

"Well, that's not so difficult," said Kaz. "There were only five people in the house."

"Yes," added Matt excitedly, "And we know all the doors and windows were locked. We can't count Constanza – so one of her four guests must be the thief!" They asked Constanza for the four names, then hurried back to Grimebusters.

"OK, we need a case file," said Matt, looking up the names in an old phone book and ripping them out. Kaz joined in, gathering up other useful-looking papers.

But nothing seemed to help much, until Kaz began to think about the torn note in her pocket. Assuming it had been sent to one of their suspects, she could figure out the meeting place it mentioned.

Who was the note sent to?
Where is the meeting place?

Allegro City Telephone directory   p384

Malloney D 17 Salero St   484 983 03
Malloney S, 14 Opera Av   785 793 48

The four suspects
Hal Gough
 - hat and raincoat
Annabelle Lotte
 - tall, brown hair
Eduardo Jones
 - long hair, flamboyant clothes
Sally Malloney
 - short, red hair

Jones D, 67 Dockside   712 378
Jones E, 3 Red Lion Yard 478 398

THE TRAITOR'S KNOT

No one knows the origin of this strang medallion, which is no in the private collectic of opera singe Constanza Smith. It thought to date back

ROGER DE FEY

the eighteenth century when the corr governor Roger de Fey ruled the city. Ind some have suggested that it may even h belonged to de Fey, and that it had some hidden significance for him. This has never been proved, and the real history and significance of the medallion remain a mystery.

THE TRAITOR'S KI

Lott A, 34 Lamp Street   558 973
Lotte A, 18 Plaza Julio   234 493

The Royal Fort is proud to announce a new exhibition: TREASURES OF ALLEGRO August 15th - 31st The main attraction will be the Allegro Crown Jewels, the city's most famous – and valuable – treasures. Normally kept under lock and key in the vaults of the fort, the Crown Jewels have not been seen by the public for twenty years. Numerous other treasures will also be on display, including the strange Traitor's Knot medallion, on loan from a private collection. Don't miss this once-in-a-lifetime exhibition!

THE ALLEGRO CROWN JEWELS

Gough A, 34 Madero Pl   682 684 39
Gough H, 13 Corneta Rd   323 452 78
Gough K, 34 Opera Av   745 452 90

GUIDE TO ALLEGRO – LEISURE CONT...

CAFÉS
(Complete list)

Café Alfonso, 45 South St
The Golden Egg, 56 Tempest Rd
The Singing Kettle, 1 Opera Av
Café Superbo, 72 Fishmarket Row
Cosimo's Cosy Caff, 35 Cathedral St
The Chip & Lettuce, 5 Long St
Isabel's Café, 26 Western Av
The Grapevine, 37 Galleon Sq
Healthy Life Café, 12 Mistero St
The Greasy Pan, 64 Broad St

Allegro Landmarks
A. The Royal Fort
B. Orlando Wharf
C. The Market Place

Healthy Life Café
12 Mistero St

ANTIQUES
(Complete list)

Curiosity Corner, 3 South St
Bygones, 41 Western Avenue
Joker's Antiques, 39 Lamp St
Junk & Clutter, 56 Broad St
Miscellany, 18 Plaza Julio

Miscellany
18 Plaza Julio

Curiosity Corner
3, South St

Suspicions

It didn't take Kaz and Matt long to decide on their next move. They would go and spy on Sally Malloney's meeting at the Singing Kettle.

They met up early the next morning. Not quite as early as planned – that old alarm clock had to go, thought Kaz – but it wasn't long after ten when they got to the café. Right away, Kaz spotted Sally, deep in conversation with a companion.

Cautiously, they crept closer, hoping to hear what the two were talking about. Kaz did manage to hear a few words – and they confirmed her suspicions about Sally. This detective business was pretty easy, really.

There's nothing to worry about – the plan can't fail. Just keep your nerve.

A few minutes later, Sally Malloney jumped to her feet, said a hasty goodbye to her companion and hurried away from the café.

"Let's follow her," whispered Matt excitedly.

They shadowed her along dim alleyways, through a bustling street market and on into the busiest part of the city.

She's heading for the market.

108

Suddenly Sally slipped through a door. Kaz and Matt followed her into a crowded warehouse.

"We'll get a better view from that balcony," whispered Matt. At the top, they watched Sally meet a shifty-looking character.

Excitedly, Matt peered through his Super-Zoom Mini-Binoculars as Sally handed something over. It was a plan of some kind – with a coded message!

What does the message say?

Chaos!

What smokescreen? What map? Whatever Sally was up to, it sounded very strange, thought Kaz, as they followed her out of the warehouse.

"We have to find out where she goes next," said Kaz. It was a good idea, but before they'd gone far, Sally headed into a maze of streets, and vanished.

"So what now?" asked Matt.

"I don't know," replied Kaz, "but I'm starving. Let's find something to eat."

An hour later, wandering back to the van, they walked right into mayhem. In front of them the Governor's Mansion was spilling out people on all sides. It seemed to be on fire!

In the middle of dodging fire hoses, Matt suddenly stopped and pointed. Kaz followed his gaze. A fireman – sprinting *away* from the mansion. Weird. Then slowly, other things began to occur to her... a lot of smoke... and the time was 1:15! Kaz began to suspect very strongly that Sally Malloney was involved in all this.

What do you think?

110

111

Undercover Investigation

Kaz and Matt raced after the suspicious firefighter, determined to find out more...

...but he jumped into a waiting van, and sped off into the distance.

"There's something weird about this fire," said Kaz. "Maybe there are clues in the Mansion."

First they'd have to get inside. In a flash, Kaz realized she had the perfect cover. She dashed off.

I've been sent by Grimebusters, fire damage specialists.

A short while later she was back, laden with buckets, mops and her vacuum cleaner.

At the entrance to the Mansion, she had no trouble getting past the guard. She hurried inside.

Kaz wandered nervously through the rooms. Strangely, there was no sign of fire, just wisps of smoke. Then she overheard three people talking. Apparently an old city map had been stolen from a safe. Well, that confirms it, thought Kaz. A map... and a smokescreen! The case against Sally looked pretty watertight.

Unfortunately, it was about to leak. A loose page from a letter caught Kaz's eye. It seemed very suspicious – but the suspect wasn't Sally Malloney!

Who was it?

113

The Plot Thickens

An hour or so later, Kaz was bringing Matt up to date. "So now we have *two* suspects," said Matt. "But which is guilty? Sally? Or Annabelle? Or maybe they're in it together," he added.

"Well I'm sure the two *crimes* are connected," said Kaz. "It makes you wonder if there'll be more…"

"Maybe they're master criminals with a master plan!" Matt broke in, getting carried away.

"Hmmm… well maybe," said Kaz. "Tell you what – let's go and visit Annabelle at Miscellany."

But when Kaz and Matt got there, they didn't just find Annabelle – Sally and Constanza were there too. Annabelle seemed to be finishing off a phone call.

Kaz and Matt listened in as Constanza and Sally said their goodbyes. Constanza's parting words sounded very suspicious indeed. This was getting more confusing by the minute! As Sally turned to climb into her car, she looked straight at Kaz and Matt.

"She's looking at us *again*," hissed Kaz, as she and Matt beat a hasty retreat.

…tomorrow… 10am… where do you want to meet?

…so the Phantom Conspiracy will be a triumph! Everything's planned down to the last detail.

When they got back to Grimebusters, Kaz and Matt were still debating whether Sally, Annabelle and Constanza could possibly *all* be in it together.

Opening the door, Kaz stumbled over a pile of papers.

"Another load of junk mail," she groaned. But then she saw something. "Oh, no – remember all that smoke at the Governor's Mansion?" she said."We just got ourselves *another* suspect!"

Who?

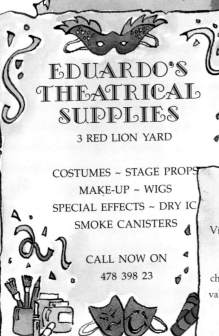

EDUARDO'S THEATRICAL SUPPLIES

3 RED LION YARD

COSTUMES ~ STAGE PROPS
MAKE-UP ~ WIGS
SPECIAL EFFECTS ~ DRY IC
SMOKE CANISTERS

CALL NOW ON
478 398 23

ALLEGRO'S
*Royal Oper
House*
IS PROUD
TO PRESENT A NE
OPERA
STARRING
*Constanza
Smith*

THE GRAPEVINE

Right next to the Royal Fort, this busy café brings you tastes from around the world. Whether you choose a full meal, or just a lunchtime snack, you can be sure of a warm welcome. Don't forget to visit our wine cellars – historic vaults which date back many centuries!

TREASURES OF ALLEGRO: *SPECIAL OFFER!*

Visit the spectacular *Treasures of Allegro* exhibition at the Royal Fort and you will automatically get free admission to any other historic building of your choice! *Treasures of Allegro,* brings together the most valuable and historic jewels in the city, with numerous loans from private collections. See the intriguing Traitor's Knot medallion, the glittering Castillo emeralds, and of course the world-famous Crown Jewels of Allegro normally kept under lock and key in the vaults. The exhibition runs from August 15th to 31st. Don't miss it!

The Allegro Crown Jewels – see them at the Royal Fort!

Kidnap!

This was ridiculous! They now had reason to suspect almost everyone who was in Marvello Mansion the previous morning.

"So who do we investigate first?" asked Matt. "Sally, Annabelle, Constanza... or Eduardo and his smoke canisters?"

Before Kaz could reply, the phone rang. It was Sally Malloney. "I'm in terrible danger," she said. "Please come at once!"

What danger? And why call us, Kaz wondered. Confused, they jumped back into the van and set off for Sally's house.

When they arrived, they were startled to see that the door had been smashed open.

Nervously, they stepped inside. In front of them, the hall was in a real mess.

"What on earth has happened?" asked Matt, staring at the smashed pictures and upturned chairs.

116

Before they could explore further, a man appeared behind them, thrust a piece of paper into Matt's hand and then ran off again. After they'd read the note, Kaz and Matt looked at each other, amazed.

"Sally Malloney's been kidnapped!" Matt exclaimed. "We must rescue her!"

"Hmmm," said Kaz. "This is all getting a little confusing. But we'd better try and find her." Luckily, with the help of the message and Kaz's map of Allegro, they could figure out exactly where Sally had been taken.

Where?

The Hotel Grande

As they made their way to the hotel, Kaz and Matt struggled to make sense of events.

"I can't understand why Sally's been kidnapped," said Matt, "but at least it means she can't be guilty of the crimes."

"I suppose not," Kaz replied. "But what about all the evidence against her? I'm totally baffled!"

It was growing dark when Kaz and Matt reached the hotel, which seemed half-derelict and run-down. "They seem very safety-conscious here," giggled Matt. "Look at all the fire escapes!" They hid behind some boxes at the back of the hotel.

"So what now?" asked Kaz. "We can't just walk in and demand to search every room."

At that moment, Matt caught a glimpse of a shadowy figure at a high window next to a flagpole. "There she is," he exclaimed. "It's Sally – up at that window."

Now they knew where they had to go. They quickly decided to climb the fire escapes and enter the room from the balcony.

Which way should they go?

We can get up there easily enough – but we'll have to climb onto the balconies as we go.

118

Rescue

Twenty minutes later, and gasping for breath, Matt and Kaz were crouching on a balcony outside the lighted room. Cautiously, they peered inside.

"There she is," hissed Kaz, pointing to a rope-bound figure in one corner. "But why is she all tied up? I thought you saw her standing at the window."

Quickly, Kaz and Matt scrambled inside and set to work on the tangle of ropes. The knots were easy enough to undo.

Thank goodness you've come!

"Please hurry," pleaded the prisoner. "My kidnappers could return at any moment!"

As soon as she was free, they all scrambled down the precarious ladders to safety.

They ran off through the rubble behind the hotel, then collapsed in a sweaty heap next to a wall. As soon as she had her breath back, Sally Malloney launched into a long and complicated explanation of whys, whats and wheres that left little room for doubt...

It certainly explained all those suspicious meetings and messages. Far from being the villain, Sally was actually trying to expose the criminals!

She even gave Kaz and Matt a coded note. "We think it was written by one of the Traitor's Knot thieves," she explained. "And now," she added, "I must scoot off. Thanks for everything!"

What does the note say?

121

Station Meeting

This gets more and more like a spy story, mused Kaz. And why didn't Sally need the note herself? "Oh well," she said, "If the Traitor's Knot thieves are going to be at the station tomorrow morning, we'd better be there too."

And so they were – along with a few hundred other people, but on time at least.

So where was the snack bar? Using a plan of the building and the coded note, they worked it out pretty quickly.

"I don't *believe* this," said Kaz, looking over at the crowded tables. "We might have cleared one suspect, but now we've gained another. Look!"

Who has she seen?

ALLEGRO STATION

BOOKS	CARDS	SNACK BAR	CHOC-OLATES	SNACK BAR	PIZZAS
SNACK BAR					NEWS
TICKET					SNACK BAR
PIZZAS	SNACK BAR	FLORIST	BOOKS	CHOC-OLATES	TOILETS

LOWER LEVEL

WAITING ROOM	FLORIST	TOURIST OFFICE	CHOC-OLATES	SNACK BAR	PIZZAS
CARDS					NEWS
NEWS					PIZZAS
PIZZAS	SNACK BAR	CHOCOLATES	FLORIST	CARDS	BOOKS

UPPER LEVEL

123

A Secret Hideout?

Annabelle Lotte – and Hal Gough! So he was mixed up in this too! Who wasn't, thought Kaz, with a sigh.

Pretty soon, the two of them got up from their table and headed through some gates.

"OK," said Kaz. "We'll follow them. We have to figure this out."

...hang on, we'll be inside in a moment...

Hal and Annabelle hurried through an engine shed to one of the office units at the back. Then Hal punched a sequence into an electronic lock.

"A secret hideout!" said Matt. "They *must* be up to something." Whatever it was, they were only inside for a few minutes before heading back into the station.

"Let's go inside and search for clues," said Matt. "Maybe we'll find some evidence against Hal and Annabelle. There's only one problem," he added, "the lock."

"Not such a problem!" said Kaz, beginning to think she was turning into an expert detective after all. "I watched Hal. The combination's 7814."

Actually, it turned out to be 8714, but it wasn't long before Kaz and Matt were inside.

Not exactly a villains' den, thought Kaz, looking around the tidy office. And after scanning a few diary pages, she was soon convinced that their two suspects weren't suspects at all…

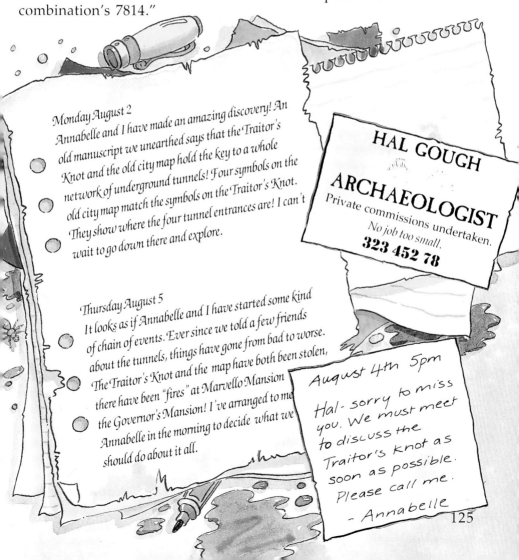

Monday August 2
Annabelle and I have made an amazing discovery! An old manuscript we unearthed says that the Traitor's Knot and the old city map hold the key to a whole network of underground tunnels! Four symbols on the old city map match the symbols on the Traitor's Knot. They show where the four tunnel entrances are! I can't wait to go down there and explore.

Thursday August 5
It looks as if Annabelle and I have started some kind of chain of events. Ever since we told a few friends about the tunnels, things have gone from bad to worse. The Traitor's Knot and the map have both been stolen, there have been "fires" at Marvello Mansion the Governor's Mansion! I've arranged to meet Annabelle in the morning to decide what we should do about it all.

HAL GOUGH
ARCHAEOLOGIST
Private commissions undertaken.
No job too small.
323 452 78

August 4th 5pm
Hal- sorry to miss you. We must meet to discuss the Traitor's Knot as soon as possible. Please call me.
- Annabelle

125

Strange Events

So Hal and Annabelle were innocent – just investigating a little bit of Allegro's history! But why arrange their meeting so secretly, wondered Kaz.

"The interesting thing about all this is the tunnels," said Kaz.

"Yes," agreed Matt. "Whoever stole the city map and the Traitor's Knot must have known about them – and was very eager to find out more. But why?"

Neither Matt nor Kaz had an answer to this, so they returned to their list of suspects.

"We think we can rule out Sally, Annabelle and Hal," Kaz began. "So that leaves Constanza and Eduardo Jones. I think it's time we went to Eduardo's Theatrical Supplies."

When they finally found it, Eduardo's was locked up and shuttered. Kaz and Matt crept around to the back, and almost stumbled straight into the middle of a very strange scene.

Two heavily disguised figures were letting themselves into Eduardo's back door. From something they said, Kaz guessed they were planning a crime with Eduardo.

126

The two men disappeared for a few moments, then re-emerged, and began loading a yellow truck with crates and boxes. Then, as Kaz and Matt crept closer, one of them pulled out a mobile phone and started to talk. Kaz and Matt strained to listen, but only caught a few words.

They did hear him mention a 'safe place' where the boxes were to be taken. And the names seemed familiar…

"I know exactly where that is!" exclaimed Kaz, suddenly.

Where is the 'safe place'?

Orlando Wharf

Clearly, Kaz and Matt had to investigate the villains' 'safe place'. They waited until the coast was clear...

...then set off for Orlando Wharf. They arrived just as the yellow truck sped off again. Now it was safe to explore the Seamist.

Cautiously, they approached the boat. They climbed onto the deck and then, finding an unlocked hatch, quickly slipped down into the main cabin. Almost at once, Matt gasped with excitement. "Look over there!" he shouted.

"The stolen map! *And* the Traitor's Knot! We've found it, Kaz!" he cried.

There it was, just sitting there. What they'd been looking for all along, and yet...

Something told Kaz this wasn't the end of the trail. Who had carried out the thefts? And why? A coded message lying next to the Traitor's Knot might help.

What does it say?

Revelations

It looked as if *another* crime was planned – some grand scheme was reaching its climax. That night, Kaz lay awake (with the Traitor's Knot and the map both safely under her pillow), going over everything in her mind.

At least they'd been right about the tunnels. They seemed to be a vital part of the plan, whatever the plan was. The coded message talked about vaults ...maybe that was important.

It was all so confusing. Who was behind it all? What were they about to steal? And why was that code vaguely familiar? With all these thoughts spinning around in her head, Kaz finally drifted off to sleep.

The next morning, Matt had a bright idea. "Let's ask Hal Gough for some help," he said. "After all, he knows more than we do about the tunnels."

They drove to Hal's house. He was surprised to see them, but said he'd try to help.

"You already seem to know as much as I do," he began. "But –"

Hal never had a chance to finish. Suddenly everything started happening at once.

First there was a ring at the front doorbell. It was Eduardo Jones. "My warehouse has been raided!" he cried as soon as he walked through the door. "When I got in this morning, whole *piles* of boxes had been taken."

All kinds of things were taken – fireworks, fake bombs, smoke canisters...

Uh oh, wrong again, thought Kaz. From the sound of it, Eduardo was innocent – and had nothing to do with the heavily disguised men at his warehouse.

Before they could find out more, there was a hammering on the door. This time it was a breathless Constanza Smith.

"Have you heard the news?" she gasped. "Someone is *blowing up* the Royal Fort! Smoke is pouring from the building this very minute! The place will burn to the ground in no time! Really, this city is a disaster area! First the Traitor's Knot was stolen, then someone committed an *outrage* at the Governor's Mansion. And now *this*!" She paused for breath.

"This must be the work of the thieves," said Kaz decisively. "Come on Matt, I've got a feeling we're about to really prove our worth!" In moments they were on their way to the Royal Fort...

Panic!

Matt and Kaz sprinted into the square and skidded to a halt, staring in amazement. Huge clouds of smoke, bangs, flashes, sparks – the Fort seemed to be having its very own firework extravaganza! Given what Eduardo had said he'd lost, it was a fair bet most of his stock was going up in flames before their very eyes.

The message they'd found on the Seamist was beginning to make sense, thought Kaz. Someone had targeted this building, for sure! And there was enough chaos and confusion here to distract an army of guards... guards... vaults... wait a minute...

"Quick!" said Kaz, thinking back to their case file and the pile of junk mail, "I've just worked out what the villains are planning to steal!"

What?

133

The Villains Strike

The Allegro Crown Jewels! The city's most priceless treasures!

"We've got to tell someone!" cried Kaz. They rushed over to a group of security guards to try and explain.

The guards weren't very impressed at first – not surprising really, given Kaz and Matt's appearance – but at last, after an exchange of radio messages, they set off at a run, with Kaz and Matt behind them.

They headed for a side entrance, then raced along darkened corridors, until they reached the vault where the Crown Jewels were kept.

One guard keyed in the code to open the door, and then gasped. The vault was empty!

With guards panicking all around them, Kaz and Matt headed straight into the vault.

"There – look," shouted Matt above the din, pointing at a gaping hole in the wall. "A doorway!"

Kaz was not surprised to find that it led directly into the network of underground tunnels.

Matt and Kaz plunged into the tunnels, which led off in different directions. Which way had the thieves gone? As Kaz reached the top of a flight of steps, she spotted a scrap of paper on the ground.

Snatching it up, she guessed it had been dropped by one of the escaping gang of villains.

Kaz and Matt quickly skimmed through the note.

At last the identity of the gang leader was clear. What was more, the city map and Traitor's Knot would tell them where the villains were heading.

Who is the leader? Where will the villains leave the tunnels?

The modern map will tell us what the building's called.

Gus:
Crimebusters are off my trail. Staging my kidnapping was a great idea! Now we can get on with the master plan. I have been into the old tunnels. Everything is perfect. After taking the jewels, we'll come out through the tunnel entrance nearest to the Fort. More instructions soon.

135

Getaway

Sally Malloney! Their first ever suspect... so she'd been guilty all along! Matt and Kaz raced back out of the tunnels, and set off above ground for the Grapevine café. But would they be in time to intercept the villains?

The café was right next to the Royal Fort, and the whole area was still in turmoil.

"Follow me," ordered Kaz, scrambling up onto a high-up balcony to get a better view.

"The thieves can't be far away," she cried, as Matt joined her. They scanned the crowded street below, trying to spot Sally and her gang.

Suddenly, Kaz let out a yell of triumph. "They're over there!" she shouted down to the guards. "Catch them!"

Can you spot the villains?

137

The Aftermath

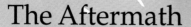

Over the next few days, Kaz and Matt read all about their exploits in the papers, and got loads of letters, including one from Sally herself! You never know, thought Kaz, maybe we haven't seen the last of her yet!

Dear Crimebusters – or should that be Grimebusters? No doubt you're feeling very pleased with yourselves. But if Gus hadn't dropped that message in the tunnels you'd never have suspected me. You really went for the kidnapping story, didn't you? Not to mention the fake coded message! No, you weren't that clever – just lucky! See you again – I promise!

Last night, intrepid investigators, Kaz Smiley and Matt Drake returned the Allegro Crown Jewels to the Royal Fort. Meanwhile, it was revealed that the building was unharmed by yesterday's events. The conspirators used theatrical smoke and other special effects to create the illusion of an explosion.

...so emerged ...y Malloney

her accomplices were behind a string of other crimes.

Police have just revealed that Sally was working for the unscrupulous art collector, Jack Smithers. He met Sally Malloney at the Singing Kettle café last Thu...

YOU ARE INVITED TO THE OPENING NIGHT
OF A NEW OPERA
THE PHANTOM CONSPIRACY
STARRING WORLD-FAMOUS SOPRANO
CONSTANZA SMITH
AUGUST 29TH 8:00PM

Do hope you can both come – after all, it was the Phantom Conspiracy that made you suspect me of terrible deeds! Thank you for everything – Constanza.

All three members of the Crown Jewels Conspiracy were taken to Allegro Central police station following their arrest outside the Royal Fort. Sally Malloney, the cunning an devio...

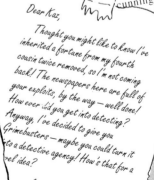

Dear Crimebusters,
Thank you for your splendid detective work! The whole city is grateful to you.
I was myself one of the few people who knew about the old tunnels – my old friend Annabelle Lotte wrote to me to tell me all about them – but I never dreamed they'd be used for a criminal plot!
Thank you once again –
Thomas Maverick
Governor of Allegro.

Dear Kaz,
Thought you might like to know I've inherited a fortune from my fourth cousin twice removed, so I'm not coming back! The newspapers here are full of your exploits, by the way – well done! However did you get into detecting? Anyway, I've decided to give you Grimebusters – maybe you could turn it into a detective agency! How's that for a ...vel idea?

love,
Mary

Clues

Pages 102-103

Look back to pages 100 and 101. Read all the notices!

Pages 104-105

Can you figure out how the pieces fit together?

Pages 106-107

Remember the message on page 105. How many of the suspects live on the same road as a café?

Pages 108-109

Five letters have been replaced by numbers.

Pages 110-111

Think carefully about the coded message on page 109.

Pages 112-113

Can you find the address of Miscellany antiques? Now check the suspects' addresses.

Pages 114-115

Remember the strange canisters found at the Governor's Mansion? Where could they have come from?

Pages 116-117

Remember where Sally lives?

Pages 118-119

Try each starting point in turn.

Pages 120-121

Try ignoring the spaces.

Pages 122-123

Look at the message on page 121.

Pages 126-127

Have you heard of the Aurora before?

Pages 128-129

Five letters have been replaced by numbers again. Which ones this time?

Pages 132-133

The message on page 129 says the villains' target is in vaults somewhere. Valuable things are kept in vaults – look back at papers on pages 107 and 115!

Pages 134-135

Remember Hal's diary on page 125. This should help you find the tunnel entrances. Use the modern map on page 117 to name the building where the thieves are heading.

Pages 136-137

They've hitched a ride.

Answers

Pages 102-103

Constanza Smith says that the leaflet was delivered 'last week'. It is now August 4, so the leaflet was delivered in July. Mary's notice on page 100, says that all leaflets delivered in July had a misprint, and came from box 4. You can see a sample leaflet stuck on this box at the bottom of page 101. It reads:

Grimebusters has become Crimebusters! Kaz has been called in as a detective, to find the thief of the Traitor's Knot.

Pages 104-105

The pieces of paper fit together as shown, to reveal this message:

> Wednesday 4th
> Need to discuss latest developments Have you planned final swoop yet? Meet me tomorrow morning at ten to make arrangements for the handover. I'll be at the café at the end of your road.
> Please be prompt.

Pages 106-107

Looking at the phone book entries and the page from the guide to Allegro, Kaz realizes that only one suspect lives on the same road as a café. It is Sally Malloney. The meeting place is the Singing Kettle café.

Pages 108-109

The vowels have been replaced by numbers. A is now 2, E is 3, I is 4, O is 5 and U is 6.
The message says: OPERATION SMOKESCREEN BEGINS AT 1:00 PM. MAP IN CABINET AT X. USE AGREED DISGUISE.

Pages 110-111

Everything fits in with Sally's coded instructions on page 109. The mansion is clouded in smoke, it's not long after 1:00 pm, and the running man Matt has noticed is holding a piece of paper that could well be a map. What's more, he is dressed as a fireman, but isn't behaving like one – is this the 'agreed disguise'?

Pages 112-113

The pieces of paper on pages 106 and 107 show that Annabelle Lotte has the same address as Miscellany antiques. She is the owner – so she wrote the note!

Pages 114-115

Eduardo Jones is clearly implicated here. The smoke canister pictured in the ad for Eduardo's Theatrical Supplies is the same as the ones on the floor at Marvello Mansion and in the man's hand at the Governor's Mansion. And there's no other Eduardo involved – the address is the same as his address in the phone book (page 106).

Pages 116-117

The route is shown here in red. It leads to the Hotel Grande.

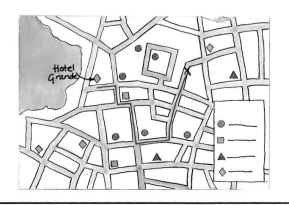

Pages 118-119

The safe, unbroken route is shown here in red.

Pages 120-121

To decode the message, Kaz and Matt first take out all punctuation marks and word spaces. Then they put capital letters in the right places, and add punctuation and spaces once again. This is what it says:

Meet me at the train station at eleven am on August sixth at the snack bar next to a chocolate shop. It is in the same row as one of the bookshops, but is not directly opposite a florist. I will be wearing my usual brown hat.

Pages 122-124

Using the station plan, and the message on page 121, Kaz and Matt work out that the meeting will take place at this snack bar.

They spot two familiar figures sitting at one of the tables. They are Hal Gough and Annabelle Lotte, circled in red.

Pages 126-127

Kaz remembers that the Aurora is the name of the houseboat she cleaned on Wednesday. In the picture on page 100, you can see that one of the other boats at Orlando Wharf is called the Aleppo. Between the Aleppo and the Aurora is the Seamist.

This must be the villains' 'safe place'.

Pages 128-129

The letters L, N, R, S and T have been replaced by numbers. L is now 2, N is 3, R is 4, S is 5 and T is 6.

The message says: HERE IS THE FINAL PLAN: WE WILL CREATE CHAOS AND CONFUSION AT TARGET BUILDING AT 11:00. THIS WILL DISTRACT GUARDS WHO KEEP VAULTS UNDER CONSTANT SURVEILLANCE. THEN WE'LL ENTER VAULTS THROUGH TUNNELS AND CARRY OUT THEFT.

Pages 132-133

From the message on page 129, Kaz knows that the villains are
intending to steal something from the vaults of a 'target building'.
The leaflets on pages 107 and 115 reveal that the Allegro Crown
Jewels are kept in the vaults of the Royal Fort. These are the most
valuable treasures in the whole city – they must be what the
villains are after!

Pages 134-135

The reference to staging a kidnap is an instant giveaway: Sally
Malloney has to be guilty!

To figure out where she and her gang are heading, Kaz and Matt
think back to Hal's diary (page 125). There are four symbols on
the old map that match symbols on the Traitor's Knot. They show
the sites of buildings with tunnel entrances.
The Royal Fort has the ☆ symbol on the old map. The nearest
entrance to it is in the building with the ⊛ symbol. From the
modern map, Kaz and Matt can name this as The Grapevine café.

Pages 136-137

Sally Malloney and
her accomplices are
riding on a fire
engine –
appropriate really,
given the disguises
they've used in the
past. They are
circled in red.

First published in 1997 by Usborne Publishing Ltd,
Usborne House, 83-85 Saffron Hill, London EC1N 8RT,
England.
Copyright © 1997 Usborne Publishing Ltd.
The name Usborne and the device are Trade Marks of
Usborne Publishing Ltd. All rights reserved.